"You amaze me, Emily,"

Carson said, grinning and shaking his head. "Most of the time you come off like a total flake. You eat pizza for breakfast and hang pictures at midnight. Then today happens, and you're suddenly a mature, in-charge person. I don't know quite what to make of you, Emily James."

"I'm not so hard to figure out. I just like to enjoy life."

"The way you didn't have a chance to do when you were growing up."

She shifted uncomfortably and took another sip of her brandy. "It's possible to have a good time on both ends of your life, you know. You might want to try it sometime."

"I just might," he said softly, his gaze slowly stroking her from head to foot, heating every place it touched.

Dear Reader,

This month, Silhouette Romance has a wonderful lineup—
sure to add love and laughter to your sunny summer days
and sultry nights. Marie Ferrarella starts us off with another
FABULOUS FATHER in *The Women in Joe Sullivan's Life*.
Sexy Joe Sullivan was an expert on *grown* women, but when
he suddenly finds himself raising three small nieces, he needs
the help of Maggie McGuire—and finds himself falling
for her womanly charms as well as her maternal instinct!
Cassandra Cavannaugh has plans for her own BUNDLE OF
JOY in Julianna Morris's *Baby Talk*. And Jake O'Connor
had no intention of being part of them. Can true love turn
Mr. Wrong into a perfect father—and husband for Cassie?

Dorsey Kelley spins another thrilling tale for WRANGLERS
AND LACE in *Cowboy for Hire*. Bent Murray thought
his rodeo days were behind him, until sassy cowgirl
Kate Monahan forced him to face his past—and her place
in his heart. Handsome Michael Damian gets more than
he bargained for in Christine Scott's *Imitation Bride*.
Lacey Keegan was only pretending to be his fiancée, but
now that wedding plans were snowballing, he began
wishing that their make-believe romance was real.

Two more stories with humor and love round out the
month in *Second Chance at Marriage* by Pamela Dalton,
and *An Improbable Wife* by debut author Sally Carleen.

Happy Reading!

Anne Canadeo

Senior Editor, Silhouette Romance

Please address questions and book requests to:
Silhouette Reader Service
U.S.: 3010 Walden Ave., P.O. Box 1325, Buffalo, NY 14269
Canadian: P.O. Box 609, Fort Erie, Ont. L2A 5X3

AN IMPROBABLE
WIFE

Sally Carleen

ROMANCE™
Published by Silhouette Books
America's Publisher of Contemporary Romance

To Abbie, Alfie, Annie, Betty, Bob, Candy, Carla, Carolyn, Cheryal, Christie, Collins, Darlene, David, Delaine, Ed, Elaine, Elizabeth, Gay, Gayle, Ginger, Glenda, Gloria, Gordon, Gus, Gwen, Jackie, Janet, Janice, Jeannie, Jim, Jody, Jon, Judy C., Judy R., Julia, Julie, Karen, Laura, Linda, Marcia, Marie, Marilyn, Mary R., Mary W., Nancy, Nora, Olga, Pat, Paula, Peggy, ReNee, Rona, Rose, Ruth, Sandy, Sharon E., Sharon H., Susan, Teri, Terry, Virginia and all my other friends.

 SILHOUETTE BOOKS

ISBN 0-373-19101-4

AN IMPROBABLE WIFE

Copyright © 1995 by Sally B. Steward

Printed in U.S.A.

Books by Sally Carleen

Silhouette Romance

An Improbable Wife #1101

Silhouette Shadows

Shaded Leaves of Destiny #46

SALLY CARLEEN

has supported her writing habit in the past by working as a legal secretary, real estate agent, legal assistant, leasing agent, executive secretary and several other things. She now writes full-time and looks upon those jobs as research for her real career of writing. A native of Oklahoma (McAlester) and a naturalized Texan (Dallas), Sally now lives in Lee's Summit, Missouri, with her husband, Max, and dog, Samantha. Her interests, besides writing, are chocolate and Classic Coke.

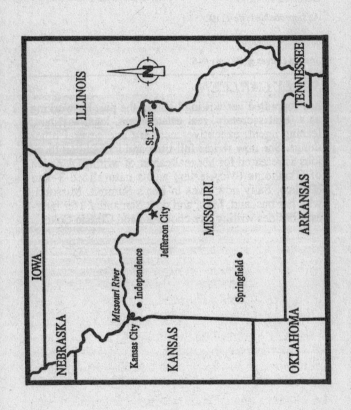

Chapter One

With a cup of coffee in one hand and newspaper in the other, Carson Thayer strolled out onto his front balcony. He took a deep breath, inhaling the scent of lilacs and fresh-cut grass as the fragrances drifted to him on the early-morning breeze.

Across the street Mrs. Johnson came down her walk in her pink chenille bathrobe and matching foam curlers. She stooped to pick up her paper, then waved to him. "Good morning, Mr. Thayer!"

"Morning," he returned. With a sigh of contentment, he settled into a wrought-iron chair half hidden in the branches of the big oak tree and set his coffee on the matching table. He should have cut the tree back last winter, but he rather liked the feeling of privacy the encroaching foliage gave him.

As he unfolded his paper and prepared to indulge in a leisurely reading, the quiet old Kansas City neighborhood suddenly exploded with shouting and honking.

He jumped, startled, and looked down. A caravan careened along his tranquil street—a caravan led by a turquoise Volkswagen Bug, followed by a red sports car with a large plant growing from the open sunroof, a yellow convertible sprouting chairs and lamps, three pickup trucks loaded with furniture, two more cars and another pickup.

He spread his paper in front of his face again, determined to ignore the intrusion until it disappeared into the distance.

It turned into his driveway.

He sighed, stood, set his paper down beside his coffee and leaned over the rail. "Are you lost?" he called down.

"Hi!" The door of the Volkswagen opened and the driver swung out her tanned legs—all ten feet of them. "It's me!"

She lifted her sunglasses and squinted up at him, full lips curved in a big smile. The morning sun lifted golden streaks from her short, straight hair. In her bright green shorts and hot pink T-shirt, she burst over him like a ray of sunshine. In spite of his irritation at the noisy invasion, he had to admit she possessed a certain dizzying charm. He couldn't help but return her smile.

"I'm sorry," he said, "but I think you have the wrong place."

Her laughter drifted up to him like sparkles from Fourth of July fireworks. "I'm Emily James. Your new tenant. I'm moving in today. Remember?"

He blinked, swallowed hard. *This* was the sedate third-grade teacher who'd answered his ad for a tenant to lease the bottom half of his duplex? This disturbing blaze of energy was going to live in his grandmother's apartment?

As if her mere presence weren't unsettling enough, the horde she'd brought with her began piling out of cars, laughing and talking, carrying lamps and plants and boxes, converging on his front porch.

He watched in horror as a child climbed out of the passenger side of the Volkswagen.

"Carson Thayer, this is Jeremy Miller." She indicated the boy.

"You didn't tell me you had a son." That wouldn't do at all. Home was his refuge. He could barely tolerate the commotion at work because he knew peace and quiet waited at home.

She tousled the boy's blond hair, and he grinned up at her.

"Jeremy is just helping me move in, like my other friends," she said.

"Emily, we could use a key here," someone called from the middle of the melee on the porch.

"Coming!" With a wave and a smile, Emily merged into the crowd.

Carson sank back into his chair, overwhelmed and smothered by the invasion. A third-grade teacher. Someone who'd live below him without causing any stir. Someone whose presence he'd never notice. He'd even told her it would be all right if she got a cat to keep her company.

How could he possibly have made such a major mistake? More importantly, how was he going to live with it? There could be little doubt this woman was going to make her presence known. And she'd signed a year's lease!

He lifted his coffee and drank deeply, but its rich warmth failed to comfort him. He searched his memory, recalling the evening she'd come over after a PTA meeting to view the property.

She'd worn a dark suit then, and her hair had been a well behaved light brown. But the evening had been dark, with no sunshine to reflect off her.

He remembered the Volkswagen parked at the curb and how he had been impressed with her thrift. In the shadows, he hadn't realized it was turquoise.

Maybe, he thought hopefully, when all the moving activity was over, she'd settle into a routine. Maybe it wouldn't be so unbearable after all. This was early Saturday morning. Of course she'd be full of energy now. But after teaching a classroom full of third graders all day, she'd come home exhausted, play classical music, flop into bed. His retreat would be inviolate.

But it was already the first of May. School would dismiss for summer vacation soon.

He took another sip of coffee and tried to reassure himself. Maybe he'd overreacted. He'd had a particularly bad week arguing with the city council while trying to keep an eye on his building contractors and making sure his grandmother was settled and happy in the retirement community. Of course he was stressed. Crowds and loud noise were the last thing he needed, and he'd just been assaulted by a heavy dose of both.

Beneath him, doors slammed and people shouted. And laughed. Everyone was laughing. What could possibly be so funny? Then he heard her sparkling laughter, distinctive even in the masses. It was beautiful, like a shower of musical rain.

But the surrounding cacophony grated on his nerves.

He stood and looked over the rail. Her friends were returning to the cars and trucks for another load. They seemed to come out in an endless stream. How many friends did the woman have? How many friends did one person need? And how long were they going to be charging in and out of his building, disturbing his peace?

With that many people, it couldn't take long to move her, he reassured himself. He'd go pick up Grandmother, take her shopping, maybe even to a movie. She was settling into her new home very well, but he didn't think she was ready to come back here to see someone else moving into her old place.

That should work out, he decided. When he got back here, his new tenant would be moved in and all would be back to normal.

"I found the CD player!" someone shouted from below. A chorus of cheers went up.

Carson moved a little faster, scarcely taking the time to rinse out his coffee cup before grabbing his key ring and fleeing downstairs. He was pretty sure he didn't want to hear the music they were planning to play.

"Oh, Emily, the hunk from upstairs is leaving!" Carla called as she came through the front door. Tendrils of Swedish ivy trailed behind her from the large hanging basket she carried.

"He'll be back. He lives here. You can hang that in the bay window in the kitchen. It already has some hooks in the ceiling." Emily dumped the contents of a box onto the hardwood floor and began to sort through it.

"Your landlord looks really familiar," Laura commented, grunting as she set down a large ceramic lamp.

"He's on the city council. You've probably seen him on the news." She scooted across the floor and began digging through another box.

"Oh, yeah. He's the one who renovated most of the houses in this area, isn't he? Civic minded and successful as well as pretty. Do you want him? If you don't, can I have him?"

Emily looked up from her rummaging. "What? Do I want him? I just met him! But you can't have him, anyway. What would your husband say?"

"Hmm. Yeah, you're right. Kevin would probably notice eventually."

Emily smiled as her friends went out to get another load. Carson Thayer was indeed a "hunk." But fooling around with your landlord, especially when he lived right above you, was on the same level as fooling around with somebody you worked with. Not a smart thing to do.

Though she had to admit, he'd made an awfully attractive picture this morning...so tall and stately against the backdrop of that tree, his bark brown hair and leaf green eyes blending with the foliage. In his immaculate white shirt, tucked smoothly into his sharply creased khaki pants, he'd looked pristine and perfect.

Which probably meant he was boring no matter how pretty the picture. "Pristine" and "perfect" were not her best friends. Not even frequent visitors. More like sinister foreigners.

"Has anybody seen the hose adapter for the water bed?" she called, returning her attention to the situation at hand.

"Is that a little white plastic gadget?" Ed asked, grunting as he set a box on the floor. "What have you got in here? Weights?"

"No, books. Romance novels. Yes, it's a little white gadget, and if I don't find it soon, I'll be sleeping on the floor tonight."

"I think Sam put it in his pocket when we were packing so it wouldn't get lost."

Rock music suddenly blasted through the essentially vacant apartment, echoing off the walls.

"Alfie! Turn that down! Sam! Where is he?"

"In your bedroom with Mary, trying to figure out how to put your water bed together the last time I saw him."

"Sam," she called, heading in the direction of her bedroom, "do you have my adapter in your pocket? Oh, dear." She paused in the doorway. "My water bed never looked like that before. You have the pieces sideways or upside down or something." Part of the pedestal was on top, part of the rails on the bottom, and an odd board hung loosely from one side.

Sam ran a hand through his shaggy hair and grinned. "Any chance you could sleep in it this way?"

"Do we have part of the kitchen table in here, maybe?" Mary contributed.

Emily peered closer. "No, I believe it's actually a shelf from my bookcase. What if we take this apart here and move it over there...." She began unscrewing, wishing she'd saved the directions.

By afternoon her new place was in total chaos, the final state before order, she decided. Boxes that were halfway unpacked with contents strewn meant part of the contents had been put away, and the rest were visible, ready to be relocated.

She dumped her underwear into the top drawer of her dresser and spread them fairly evenly. Lifting one corner, she shoved carefully, then raised the entire drawer to just the right angle and jiggled it in. Someday maybe she'd try to fix it so it would work easier. Though it would never move smoothly like the new, vapid drawers that slid on rollers.

She patted the scarred surface and smiled at her mottled reflection in the ancient mirror. Old and warped was better than new and vapid in her bqok any day.

The doorbell chimed. Pizza delivery. She snatched up her wallet and dashed through the house, leaping over boxes and shoving Sam aside in her efforts to reach the door first.

"You order five large pizzas?" the teenager on the front porch asked.

She paid the youth, slapping Sam's hand as he reached around her and tried to pay first. "Just take the pizzas," she urged him. "Feeding you is the least I can do after all this work everybody's done for me."

Sam kissed her cheek as he juggled the cardboard boxes. "For once you're right. Feeding us *is* the least of the things you do for your friends."

Emily felt the warm glow Sam's words evoked rise to her cheeks and knew she was blushing. Fortunately he'd already moved on. "Pizza in the kitchen!" he called to the house at large.

Jeremy bounced out of the bedroom Emily had designated as her office. "Did you get anchovy and jalapeño?"

"I sure did. A large one just for you and me." She wrapped one arm around the boy's shoulders. "How's it coming with the computer?"

He shrugged and grinned sheepishly. "It's up and running. I've just been . . ."

"Testing it?" she supplied.

"Yeah. You've got some really neat games."

The doorbell rang again.

"Maybe I gave the delivery boy the wrong amount. Go find our pizza. Sodas are in the big ice chest."

Jeremy darted away with the superfluous energy of a ten-year-old, and she returned to the door.

Carson "The Hunk" Thayer stood on the porch beside a short elderly woman with white hair in a wedge cut. She looked stylish and elegant in her beige cotton pantsuit. Her face was creased with many deep lines, but they all seemed to flow upward, giving her an impish expression that belied her obvious age.

"I'm Celia Thayer." The woman extended a well-manicured hand. "You must be Emily James."

"Yes, I am." Emily shook her hand, finding the older woman's grip to be cool and dry and surprisingly firm. "Come in." She stood back and held the door open.

The woman stepped inside without hesitation.

Carson followed . . . reluctantly, it seemed. "This is my grandmother. She wanted to meet you and see the place. She lived here until a few weeks ago." Emily could tell from the edge of irritation in his tone that he had come under protest. "I hope you don't mind."

"Of course I don't mind." But as Mrs. Thayer looked around at the disorder, Emily mentally cringed. Carson's grandmother had probably kept an immaculate home; Emily must seem like not only a usurper, but a messy usurper. Though her untidy habits rarely bothered her, she found that she didn't want to disappoint this woman with laughter in every line of her face. "I haven't got everything put away yet," she apologized.

"It's fine," Mrs. Thayer said. "Nice, actually." She smiled up at her grandson. "I like your Emily."

Emily followed Mrs. Thayer's gaze and was surprised to see a look of relief cross Carson's chiseled features. He had been more worried than she about his grandmother's reaction.

"Carson tried to keep me away from here today, but I love this place. I lived here for ten years. I had to see what was happening to it, and I approve. You'll keep it alive." Her twinkling gaze swept the disorder of the room, pausing at the dining room door from which loud talking, laughter, and spicy odors emanated.

Emily smiled. The woman hadn't said she'd keep the apartment clean—just alive. "I know I'm going to love it here. My last place was a tiny apartment. This is so spacious and open, and I have a guest room for my friends."

"Thank you very much for letting us look," Carson said, taking his grandmother's arm.

"Oh, don't leave yet. Come join us for pizza," Emily invited impulsively. She had felt an immediate camaraderie with the older woman—maybe partly because Mrs. Thayer had approved of her unstructured life-style!—and surely it would be all right to invite her "hunky" landlord to stay if his grandmother came along.

"Why, thank you," Mrs. Thayer said happily.

At the same time Carson refused with a polite, "No, thank you."

Mrs. Thayer took Emily's arm with her free hand and urged them both toward the kitchen. "You have some lovely furniture. That's a beautiful china cabinet in the corner over there. Not going to store your china in the living room, are you?"

"No, that's for my knickknacks. If I keep them behind glass, I don't have to dust them all the time."

"Grandmother, you can't eat pizza!" Carson protested.

"Certainly I can. I had my dentures relined last week."

"But what about your cholesterol?"

"What about it? I'm eighty-four years old. How much longer do you think I'm going to live, anyway? Oh, and you have the good kind of cola. All they keep in the machines at that place where I live now is that other stuff. Hello, everybody. I'm Celia Thayer. Please call me Celia."

Emily introduced Carson and Celia to the roomful of noisy people. Her friends immediately made room at the long table for the newcomers.

Carson looked a little uncomfortable, but Sam handed him a piece of pepperoni pizza on a paper plate and began talking to him. He'd be bound to feel at home in no time. Sam had that effect on people.

Emily smiled happily as she squeezed in between Jeremy and Celia. Pizza, friends and "the good kind of cola." What more could anybody ask for?

Carson took a bite of the greasy pizza and wished fervently for a beer rather than a soft drink. He should be—and he was—pleased that his grandmother was happy. He'd been concerned about her reaction to seeing someone else in her old home.

But he couldn't relax with so many people and so much noise. The small room was absolutely full of bodies, and everybody was talking at once. This was worse than being at work—at least the chaos there had a purpose. This was nothing but an invasion of his space.

The young man sitting next to him was saying something about the issues the city council was working on. But with all the distractions, Carson had to make a real effort to concentrate on his words.

Across from him, Grandmother took a big bite, cheese stringing for several inches. She and his new tenant exchanged glances and laughed uproariously.

He didn't see anything funny. What he did see was the plaque building up in his grandmother's arteries.

He tried to focus his attention on the young man beside him, give him a quasi-rational reply. What was the man's name? Usually he remembered every name in a party of a hundred, but this raucous activity had his mind spinning.

"You have some very good ideas," Carson said. "I know I won't remember all of them. Would you mind very much writing me a letter just to refresh my memory? Here, let me give you my card."

The man beamed as he accepted the card, and Carson breathed a sigh of relief. He'd managed to salvage the situation without upsetting anyone.

"Sam!" Carson and the young man turned at the sound of his grandmother's voice. *Sam*. Yes, that was his name.

"Emily says you have a race car."

"Sort of. It's really just an old dragster."

"Can I come watch the next time you race?"

"Sure you can!"

Carson gaped at his grandmother. Now she wanted to go to a drag race? She really was losing her faculties. He'd persuaded her to go to that retirement community just in time. He couldn't be around all day to look after her, and evidently she needed continual supervision.

Beside her, Emily munched on pizza and looked thrilled with the whole situation. He'd have to talk to her later, let her know how fragile Grandmother was...physically and mentally.

"You can come along, too," Emily invited. She smiled at him, and a ray of sunshine somehow found its way past the branches of the trees and through the dining room window. It danced and flashed on the gold hidden in her perfectly ordinary light brown hair and eyes. Did she attract sunshine like a magnet or did she manufacture it?

He shook his head to dispel the irrational thought.

"No?" she asked at the gesture.

"No what?"

"You don't want to come to the races with Celia and me?" She tilted her head to one side questioningly.

"Carson, don't be a stick-in-the-mud. He gets that from his mother, not from my side of the family, I assure you." Celia took another piece of pizza.

"Well, he doesn't have to come if he doesn't want to."

"Emily," Carson said, then cleared his throat. The word had come out in a pleading tone. "Emily, I'd like to talk to you later, if I might."

"Oh, Carson, don't go telling her how senile you think I am." Celia reached for the salt shaker and added more. *How could anyone add salt to pizza?*

"I don't think you're senile at all. Your body just isn't what it used to be." He resisted the urge to take the shaker away from her.

"Neither is yours," she replied archly. "And I, for one, am glad. I got awfully tired of changing your diapers and powdering your—"

"Grandmother!"

But the damage was done. Emily, Sam and Jeremy immediately burst into laughter with Grandmother joining them. He could hear the story being repeated for the benefit of those at the ends of the table who might have missed some gory detail. Soon everyone was laughing.

Beside him, Sam stood and raised his glass high. "To our new friends, Celia and Carson, and their ever-changing bodies."

"Hear, hear!" Everyone clapped and whistled, and Sam sank down again, patting him on the back.

Carson forced himself to smile, to take the bantering in the way he knew it was intended.

Then his eyes locked with Emily's. Emily, the talking, the music, all seemed to blend together and the racket burst inside him, invading his body, jarring his entire being with a cadence that beat rhythmically albeit in a wild, out-of-control way. His blood raced and bounced through his veins, pounded in his ears like a drum. He had an insane urge to leap up and begin dancing, to grab this strange, exciting woman and—

He gulped and his glass slid from his grasp, spilling ice and liquid on the table. Before he could do anything about the accident, hundreds of napkins, or so it seemed, rushed to the rescue, Emily's among them. He jerked away, afraid to touch her tanned fingers.

Not after he'd been getting aroused just looking at her.

"Grandmother, we really need to go."

"Where, dear?"

"What?"

"Where is it we need to go?"

"To the movies." He blurted the first thing that came into his head.

She shrugged, drained her glass, set it down and stood. "Thank you, Emily, for inviting us into your home. It's been a pleasure meeting all of you."

"Please come back again," Emily invited, and Carson heard the sincerity in her voice, saw the welcoming glow in her eyes. "Both of you."

He nodded noncommittally. She meant well. She couldn't help being a major irritant.

"I'll get that letter in the mail right away," Sam said, offering his hand.

"I'll look forward to receiving it." As he shook Sam's hand, he found himself wondering if the man was more to Emily than just a friend. He had sort of taken on the duties of host, entertaining the newcomers.

Then he had to wonder at himself for wondering. Certainly he had no interest in a woman who made him a nervous wreck.

At the door Emily hugged his grandmother goodnight. To his immense relief and surprising disappointment she didn't try to repeat the performance with him.

Instead she offered her hand. And that was almost enough to do him in.

Her fingertips curled around his in the perfectly usual, accepted manner, but the effect was decidedly sensual. He looked at her in surprise and saw the same disconcerted desire on her face.

He shook briefly, releasing her hand quickly lest he should hold it too long, and escaped out the door... onto the quiet serenity of the porch.

"She's very pretty," Grandmother said, and he wondered how much of the tension she'd picked up on. A few years ago he'd have been willing to bet she hadn't missed a thing. But now...

"She's very hyper," he said gruffly. "She's an ulcer waiting to happen." And she wasn't going to happen to him.

Chapter Two

The light pried Emily's eyes open. For a moment she felt disoriented. The window shouldn't be on that side of the room. Then she remembered and smiled. Her first morning in her new home—a spacious three-bedroom duplex with a yard and a rent she could afford...plus two new friends.

Well, at least Celia showed definite signs of becoming a friend. She wasn't so sure about her landlord. Her first instinct about him had apparently been right. He seemed pretty scrunched up inside and very uncomfortable around her friends. In fact, she wasn't sure if Carson Thayer was ever comfortable.

Attractive as he might be physically—and she had to admit, in the privacy of her thoughts only, that he possessed a certain charisma—it would never do to get involved with him. Why, he was probably the type who wouldn't want her friends to come along on their honeymoon!

She laughed to herself, stretched languorously and noted the angle of the sun coming through the half-open blinds. She must have slept ten hours. But after they'd all stayed up Friday night packing then moved on Saturday, she'd be willing to bet she wasn't the only one who'd had to play catch-up on sleep.

She rolled out of bed, slipped on a T-shirt and cut-offs and staggered into the kitchen. Taking a cola from the refrigerator, she popped the tab, took a long, fizzy drink and gazed out the window over the sink at the tall trees and the two colorful lilac bushes in her backyard. Her one-bedroom apartment had been on the third floor of a small building where the only grass grew between the cracks in the sidewalk.

Okay, so maybe the yard wasn't all hers, but her landlord lived upstairs with two balconies, one front and one back. She'd likely be spending more time out there than he would.

Celia must have spent a lot of time outside when she'd lived here, Emily reflected. Well-tended rose canes covering the two trellises on the back fence promised loads of fragrant blossoms. A honeysuckle vine crept along one side of the fence. On the other side irises bloomed in colorful profusion. But several flower beds sat empty, nothing sprouting from their well-tended earth.

Emily sighed, a trace of sadness pervading her day. Undoubtedly Celia really loved this place. Moving to a retirement community must have been a tough decision. She herself had only been six years old but she could still remember the pain of loss when her parents had died and she'd been torn from her home and stuck in an impersonal orphanage.

She'd see to it that Celia always felt welcome to visit. Maybe they could plant some flowers together.

Surveying the contents of her refrigerator, she smiled as she found half a dozen pieces of leftover pizza. Cola and pizza—her favorite breakfast. At the orphanage and in foster homes, she'd had to eat what she was offered—milk and cereal, pancakes, bacon and eggs or other traditional fare. She'd always promised herself that, when she grew up, she'd have pizza and cola for breakfast whenever she wanted.

She heated a couple of pieces in the microwave oven then headed out to survey the front yard. The lilac bushes spread their delicate fragrance all the way around the house. She took a deep breath and sat down on the steps to enjoy her breakfast in the sunshine and spring breezes.

A Sunday paper lay in the driveway. Of course Carson would have a subscription. He wasn't the type to walk down to the corner on an as-needed basis.

She'd go inside in a few minutes, get some change and go down to the corner. But Carson's paper was right in front of her, and since he wasn't up yet, surely he wouldn't mind if she just peeked at the comics. When she finished, she'd put it all back together so he'd never notice the difference and then take it up to him.

But she'd just gotten it all unfolded and begun to read the comics when she heard footsteps coming down the stairs. The door from the upstairs apartment swung open. Carson Thayer stepped out, wearing white shorts with crisp pleats and a white knit shirt with an embroidered emblem on the left side.

"Good morning," she greeted, trying hurriedly to refold the paper.

"Good morning. It's a beautiful day, isn't it? Are you getting settled in all right?" He barely looked at her as he passed, his gaze focused in the distance . . . looking for his newspaper, no doubt.

"Uh, I sort of borrowed your paper." She held one sheet out, trying to straighten it. The blasted thing was like a map; it refused to go back into the original folds. "I was going down to the corner, but it was so comfortable here, and I thought, well, it's not like a newspaper loses anything by being read before." She made an effort to chuckle nonchalantly, but it came out sounding phony even to her own ears.

She didn't quite know why she felt intimidated. He wasn't glaring at her, actually. His expression was more mystified than anything else as the comics, taking on a life of their own, leapt from her suddenly clumsy fingers to the ground. She leaned over to pick them up, crumpling them in the process, and the rest of the sections slid from her lap to the sidewalk.

She grabbed for the business pages just as Carson reached down. Her head bumped his, and they both jerked back to the accompaniment of a ripping sound.

His eyes widened and his nostrils flared. *Now* he was getting angry, she thought, and she didn't blame him.

"They sure do use flimsy paper these days," she said lamely, handing him the other half. "Look, I'll be happy to come up and tape it back together. Or better yet, I'll go get you a new one."

"No, no." He stepped to the side, away from her. "That's okay, really."

"Oh, be careful—"

His foot landed directly in the middle of her pizza. He jerked backward and turned over her cola. His white loafer looked pretty gross.

"Let me get a paper towel." She started for the door.

"What in heaven's name is this stuff?" He stood on one leg, holding the offending foot in the air and glaring at her. Yes, he was definitely glaring now.

"Pizza. Anchovy jalapeño pizza and a soft drink." She raised her chin a little defiantly. So she'd messed up his paper. He'd ruined her breakfast. She was entitled to a little indignation herself.

"Did your friends leave this mess here yesterday?" His eyes blazed and his chest heaved ominously.

She crossed her arms and returned his glare, her own anger erupting at the unfair attack on her friends. "You needn't worry. My friends wouldn't leave a mess on your property. That happens to be my *breakfast* you just ruined."

He reached down and plucked an anchovy from his shoe, then looked back at her, the mask of anger changing to a fascinated horror.

"I'd better go get that paper towel," she mumbled, darting inside the screen door.

She made it back to the porch with a roll of towels in time to see his bare foot disappear inside the other door. Uneven steps mounted the stairs.

All evidence of her breakfast had been tidily removed. With a sigh, she went back inside. It was a good thing she had no designs on Carson. She didn't think she'd made a very good impression this morning.

She popped open another cola and shuffled through the pizza boxes until she found another piece. She'd best stay inside to eat. Or maybe she could sit on the back stoop....

The phone rang and her mood instantly brightened. Talking to a friend would cheer her up.

"Hello?"

"Emily, it's Celia."

"Oh, Celia! You'll never believe what I just did to your grandson. I'm sure he's going to evict me before I even get unpacked!"

As she related the story, Celia burst into laughter. "You offered to tape his paper back together?"

Emily giggled. It was kind of funny, she supposed, now that it was all over. "I really ought to go buy him a new one."

"Nonsense! He didn't offer to replace your breakfast, did he? Oh, what I wouldn't give for a picture of him standing there with tomato sauce and anchovies on his spotless white shoe!"

"Holding one anchovy by its little tail...or maybe by its little head." Emily joined in Celia's laughter. "Then he went upstairs with one foot bare, carrying his shoe, I suppose."

"You've made my day. I don't know when I've had so much fun. And I'm glad my stodgy grandson stepped in your breakfast before you got a chance to eat because I called to invite you to brunch. Have you ever been to Stephenson's Sunday buffet? We need to go there with a hearty appetite."

"That sounds terrific! What time, and how do I get over to pick you up?"

After getting directions, Emily hung up the phone, delighted by the prospect of seeing Celia again. She'd spend the morning with her new friend, then in the afternoon she'd promised to take Jeremy to the park.

But right now she'd best run down to the corner and get Carson Thayer a new paper. That was the fair thing to do.

When she came back, she saw him sitting on the balcony drinking coffee and holding together pieces of torn newsprint. He didn't look up, and she resisted an urge to shout and wave the paper at him. Instead, she stood circumspectly on the porch and rang the doorbell.

He came down the stairs wearing different shoes. In the shadows of the entryway, her eyes accustomed to the bright sun, she couldn't read his expression as she handed him the mint-condition paper.

"Thank you," he said. "Though it really wasn't necessary." His words were stiff and formal, but then he cleared his throat and softened his tones. "We could both sit down here and share it, if you'd like. Have another cup of coffee."

It was definitely an olive branch. Though she really didn't want to risk touching this new copy, she did need to make peace. She'd be careful not to read anything until he'd been over it first.

"What time is it?" she asked.

He checked his gold wristwatch. "Three minutes after eight."

That gave her plenty of time before she had to get dressed for brunch. "Okay, sure. I'll just go inside and get another cola and some chairs."

"I'll be happy to bring down a pot of coffee. It's a very good blend. I grind it myself."

She smiled up at him. He'd offered to share his special coffee. That was really sweet. She hated coffee, but...

"Thank you. I'll get a cup and meet you back here."

On the other hand, maybe he wasn't being so nice after all. Maybe he knew how she felt about the stuff and was punishing her for her earlier sins.

Nah, how could he know that?

Maybe Sam told him yesterday.

The screen door swung shut behind her.

Well, she'd take her punishment, drink the bitter brew and have a cola to chase it with. Then things would be fine between her and her landlord.

She brought out two chairs, carefully positioning hers next to the rail just in case the coffee was so awful she couldn't drink it. Plants thrived on it, she'd heard. She set an open soft drink out of sight beside her chair.

He came down almost immediately with a thermal pitcher and a small folding table, both of which he set between them. She watched in fascination as he poured, measuring out precisely the same amounts for both of them.

Stifling a gag reflex, she focused away from the steaming black stream and on to the person doing the pouring. His arms and legs as they left the smooth white confinement of clothes were muscular, hard-looking, with dark hairs curling in disarray. She was surprised he didn't mousse and comb them into obedience. Those rebellious hairs provided a stark contrast to his carefully controlled appearance. She had to resist an urge to reach over and run her fingers through them, over the ridges and valleys of muscles and tendons—

"Here you go."

"Thank you." She pulled her wandering attention back to its proper place and accepted the proffered cup. He smiled warmly, his expression expectant, awaiting her response.

She sipped cautiously. "One of the best cups of coffee I've ever had," she declared emphatically. Since she'd never had more than a few tastes in her life, that much was true.

It was worth it. He beamed happily.

But she didn't care to repeat the experience. Next week she'd get her own newspaper if she had to walk five miles in the snow to do it.

"Would you like the comics again, or did you finish with them?" he asked, sorting through the sections.

"Oh, yes, I finished ... with all the good ones, that is. I think I'll just sit here and enjoy the beautiful morning and—" she swallowed hard as she prepared to lie outright "—and this terrific coffee." She set the cup on the rail beside her.

As soon as his attention was buried in newsprint, she picked up her cup, tilting it over the rail so part of the contents sloshed out, then pretended to take a drink. After a surreptitious sip of cola, she leaned back and relaxed. Except for the coffee, this wasn't so bad. She could handle sitting on the porch with Carson Thayer first thing in the morning. Well, second thing, actually. Their earlier rendezvous down here hadn't turned out so hot.

She stole a glance at him. He looked like a model posing for an ad for the perfect Sunday morning.

She stretched luxuriously, dumped some more coffee and lifted her legs to the rail. Yes, this was a lovely way to begin the week.

Carson took a deep breath as Emily raised her legs, inhaling slowly so she wouldn't notice. The woman was only average height; so why did she seem to have extraordinarily long legs? Long, tanned legs. He knew tanning was detrimental to one's health, but it sure did look good on her.

He'd invited her to sit with him in an effort to maintain civil relations since she now lived below him . . . at least, that was the reason he'd given himself. But, he had to admit, being with her when she was quiet was most pleasant.

Actually *pleasant* was an inadequate word.

"Would you like more coffee?" he asked, folding the paper in his lap, refusing to consider what the *adequate word* might be.

"Oh, no, thanks. I have to watch my caffeine."

He nodded. That was sensible of her. "So, you teach third grade? Is that something you always aspired to or just sort of fell into?"

She smiled, her eyes a dark, antique gold. Even in the shade, streaks of gold shone in her short hair. "Something I always aspired to. Well, not specifically third grade. Any grade. I love children. Having a roomful at once is like a dream come true."

Carson chuckled. "Most teachers dread that, don't they?"

She swung around, planting her bare feet firmly on the wooden porch. "If they do, they should teach correspondence school and stay away from the kids. Childhood is a time of magic. We adults owe it to them to keep it that way."

He elected not to tell her that he disagreed; that he'd been fortunate enough to have rational parents who presented the world to him realistically. "Is Jeremy one of your students?" he asked instead.

She nodded, her expression clouding. "A former student. He was in my class last year. Jeremy's home life isn't the best. Not the worst, I suppose. His mother doesn't abuse him or anything, but she's single and busy and pretty much ignores him."

"And you try to take up the slack." That was admirable, he thought as he poured more of his special blend for himself. He leaned back in his chair, savoring the warm, rich taste, the quiet morning, and the peaceful relationship he was forging with his new tenant. Maybe this was going to work out after all.

She shrugged, crossing her sleek legs. The skin on his back warmed with the thought of how those limbs would feel wrapped— "The road runs both ways," she said, diverting his attention back. He struggled to remember what they'd been talking about. "Don't you get as much as you give from taking care of Celia?" she continued. "Oh!" She leaned abruptly forward, grabbing his wrist with her slim, tanned fingers, turning his watch toward her. "I need to run. I don't want to be late for brunch with her."

"Brunch with who?" She released him, but he could swear he felt slight tingles where her fingers had touched his skin.

"Celia. Want to come along?" She bounced up, standing in front of him.

"You invited my grandmother to brunch?" Just when they'd been getting along so well, he'd discovered she was again intruding abrasively into his life.

"No, she invited me, but I'm sure she won't mind if you join us."

If Grandmother had wanted him along, she'd most certainly have asked him. "Where are you going?"

"Stephenson's. She says they have a wonderful buffet."

Carson clenched his fists in his lap. No wonder she hadn't invited him. "For you, maybe. But Grandmother has to watch her diet. She's eighty-four years old. I'd like to see her reach eighty-five."

Emily's smile turned beatific. "You must love her very much. Are your parents dead?" She leaned over, laid one cool hand on his right cheek and briefly pressed her soft lips to the other one. "I promise to take good care of her."

She walked away, rounded derriere encased in faded denim swaying atop those incredible legs. The warmth of her lips and fingers still lingered on his cheeks.

"My parents are fine. They just bought a new house in Mission Hills. They're very busy," he blurted, but she'd already gone inside, closing the door behind her.

He didn't like this association with his grandmother. True, Emily had promised to "take good care of her." But from what he'd seen of Emily James so far, he wasn't sure he trusted her definition of "good care."

Emily stumbled out of her car in the restaurant parking lot.

When she'd picked up Celia, the woman had sounded incredibly wistful as she'd admired Emily's car and told her how much she'd always enjoyed driving. Now Carson thought she was too old, and they'd sold her car.

Naturally, Emily offered to let her drive, and now she knew one of the reasons Carson worried about his grandmother. In the little car, she'd managed to terrorize at least a dozen people along the way, including her passenger.

"That was fun," Celia said, coming around and handing her the keys. "I haven't driven a stick shift in years."

"You handled that part very well. It was when you pulled in front of that semi with six inches to spare that I got a little worried."

"Well, the man was driving much too slow. And, as you said, I had a good six inches to spare." They walked through an archway covered with wisteria vines. "Isn't this lovely?"

Emily couldn't argue that the truck had been creeping along...driving the speed limit in the left lane. She'd have done the same thing. But...

Celia paused just outside the door and turned back to Emily. "Now, don't worry. In sixty-odd years of driving, I've never had an accident."

"Never?"

"Well..." Celia's gaze drifted over Emily's head as if searching for something, then returned, her expression decidedly impish. "Never one that was my fault. Not really."

They both burst into giggles.

"I thought I was never going to stop laughing when you sailed around that jerk combing his hair in the sports car with the vanity plates *STUD*. I'll bet that woke him up, being passed by an old Volkswagen." Emily pushed open the restaurant door and they entered the hallway.

The host showed them to a white-clothed table and took their drink orders for coffee and cola.

"'Old Volkswagen,'" Celia repeated, one thin eyebrow arched. "What kind of engine have you got in that thing?"

"I don't know. It died a few years ago, and Sam fixed it for me."

"Sam of the race car?"

"Dragster."

"Uh-huh." Celia nodded knowingly, and they shared a suppressed giggle. "Don't tell Carson."

"If you don't tell him I let you drive."

Celia stood and waved a negligent hand. "We have to take care of Carson. He gets stressed much too easily. Let's go find some food."

They started through the line, and Emily watched in fascination as Celia piled some of everything onto her plate—smoked ham, chicken, beef. . . .

"You seem very close to Sam," Celia said, maneuvering a piece of smoked pork in between the ham and chicken.

"Very. He's my brother."

"Your brother?" Celia added a scoop of fluffy omelet. "Odd. You don't look anything alike."

"Well, he's not my blood brother. He's more like a foster brother." She didn't want to explain the whole thing while going through the buffet line.

"You're not romantically involved, then?" Celia pursued, piling fried potatoes onto her already heaping plate.

That question almost took Emily's attention away from Celia's astonishing pile of food. "Romantically involved with Sam?" she exclaimed. "I love him with all my heart, but, good heavens, no. He's my brother—my dear, sweet, kind, bossy, pushy brother."

Celia nodded. "I see. I could tell the two of you were very attached to each other."

They moved on through the line, Celia's curiosity apparently satisfied.

"Carson said you were on some kind of diet," Emily protested as Celia loaded a second plate with desserts.

"Carson would like me to observe the old 'if it tastes good, spit it out' diet, but I've been an adult for more years than he has. I can make my own decisions. When I was young, I had to watch my hips. Now I do as I please." She took a second apple fritter. "My grandson's very handsome."

"Yes, he is," Emily agreed. Oh, dear. All the questions about Sam and now she'd brought up Carson. She hoped Celia wasn't going to attempt matchmaking between Carson and her. Handsome he might be, but terribly private and solitary as well as *pristine* and *perfect*. Not to mention that he liked to drink—and share—his atrocious coffee.

"He has a heart of gold and a brilliant mind," Celia continued. "It's just too bad no one ever taught him to have fun, and it's too late now."

Emily breathed a sigh of relief. "For a minute there I thought you were going to ask me to take on the task of teaching him."

Celia laughed gaily and started back toward their table balancing her two loaded plates. "No, of course not. I tried when he was growing up." She shook her head and smiled ruefully. "He's so much like his mother. I'm afraid it would take a miracle to make Carson lighten up. He's quite hopeless."

"I imagine you're right about that," Emily agreed, though it made her a little sad to think of giving up on anyone, especially someone with a "heart of gold and a brilliant mind"... and muscular, hairy, gorgeous arms and legs.

They found their table and sat down.

Celia regarded her fondly. "You remind me so much of myself when I was young. Then I married Edgar and settled down. Don't get me wrong—he was a kind, caring man, and I loved him dearly. But he was more than a little boring. Since he wouldn't do things with me, I soon found myself not doing the things I enjoyed anymore." She cut off a bit of smoked chicken, then raised her pale green gaze to Emily. "I fear Carson has his genes, not to mention Regina's. That's his mother. She thinks winning a bridge game or finding a new color of nail polish is the ultimate in excitement."

Emily bit into a flaky croissant and watched Celia eat ecstatically. *Celia's grandson also has her genes.* The thought raced unbidden across her mind. She shoved it away. She'd long ago learned the hard way that trying to change someone's outlook when they didn't want it changed only resulted in frustration.

"What about his father? Your son?" She only asked to make conversation, she assured herself, not because she was interested in finding out how deeply rooted Carson's stodginess was.

"I had hopes for Stephen," Celia admitted between bites. "But after he married that woman..." She shook her head and took another bite of pork chop, chewing almost angrily. "She didn't really want children. They make noise and mess up the house and disrupt schedules. So she saw to it that Carson was never a child. They treated him like an adult. Took him to the theater and symphonies while other kids were playing baseball and listening to rock music. Regina's house was always immaculate, always quiet and always boring."

"That's too bad." Emily felt her heart go out to the quiet, serious child Carson had been. Maybe he'd had the home and family she hadn't, but he'd been cheated of his childhood, too. But she was making up for lost time, having fun. Now that she was an adult, she could do what she wanted.

And, she reminded herself, Carson was also an adult who could do what he wanted. His idea of fun just differed from hers.

"This ham is wonderful," Celia enthused. "Did you get some?"

"I think it's here somewhere." Emily groaned as she surveyed the mound of food. "After I eat all this, I have to take Jeremy to the park to play football. I may die."

"Jeremy? Did I meet him yesterday?"

"Yes, the blond-haired kid. He's very bright, extremely sensitive as gifted children frequently are, and—" She shrugged. "He's just a really neat kid."

"You like children." It wasn't a question.

"If I didn't, I'd kill them some days." Emily tried the fluffy omelet. If she ate one bite of everything on her plate and two or three bites of the things she liked ...

"I always wanted a large family, but there was only Stephen." Celia cut a chunk of beef. She sounded quite matter-of-fact, not at all self-pitying, and that attitude gave Emily the courage to confide in her new friend.

"I want a large family. But I want to adopt. Not babies, older children. My parents died when I was six, and I grew up in an orphanage and foster homes, including two years with Sam and his parents. There are so many unwanted children out there, it seems almost cruel to bring any more into the world until those already here are taken care of and loved."

She hesitated. Celia had said she'd wanted a large family. Now all she had was a son who lived in the elite suburb of Mission Hills in a quiet, immaculate new house, and a stuffy grandson. Perhaps she'd enjoy sharing Emily's self-made family. "Would you like to come to the park with us?" she invited. "You don't have to play football...."

Celia's wrinkles tilted upward. "I'd love to. Can we go by my place so I can change first?"

"Of course. We'll go by your home, then pick up Jeremy, and you two can get acquainted while I change."

"Yes," Celia agreed. "I'd like that."

Carson was sitting at his computer, beside his office window, when Emily's ridiculous car turned into the driveway. He hadn't really been watching for them, but he was glad they were back. For no good reason, he breathed a sigh of relief when his grandmother climbed out.

But what on earth was she wearing? Those old gray sweats she wore to clean the house and work in the garden? Surely she hadn't gone out to eat dressed like that!

He turned away from the window and rushed downstairs.

"Hello, sweetheart," she greeted him as he burst through the door onto the porch.

"Did you wear that to the restaurant?"

"Why?"

"Huh? Why, what?"

"Why do you need to know, dear? Does it matter?" She patted his cheek. "I'll come by and visit later, but right now I have to go. I'm spending the afternoon with Emily and Jeremy."

He bit his lip, refraining from further comment. He'd gotten her into that center just in time. She was starting to become incoherent. He bent down and kissed her crepe-paper cheek. "I'll grill some chicken for dinner."

She left him with a wave, disappearing into the other door, and for a sweet, fleeting moment it seemed as if things were the same as they'd been for ten years. He'd seen her go through that door so many times, often wearing those or similar faded sweats.

His jaw clenched as he made himself face reality. Things were not the same. And he was going to have to talk to Emily, make sure she understood how much his grandmother had changed, how much she'd aged, how fragile she was.

He went upstairs and forced himself to return to the task of getting caught up on the records for his construction business. Being on the city council took a lot of time, but he couldn't afford to let his business go.

A few minutes later, at the sounds of a door slamming and people shouting, he looked down.

Emily dashed out in her frayed cutoffs and threw a football to Jeremy as he streaked across the yard. The boy caught it, turned, yelled something, drew back his arm and let fly.

Not a bad throw, Carson thought as his gaze followed the arc of the ball . . . right into the arms of his grandmother as she ran across the yard!

Chapter Three

Carson raced downstairs just in time to see his grandmother crawling into the turquoise turtle. He grabbed her arm and pulled her back, turning her to face him.

"Are you all right?" he demanded.

She looked down at his fingers. "I was fine until you nearly broke my arm." She raised one eyebrow. "Perhaps you're the one who needs additional care. Maybe you should be going to the retirement home instead of me. You've been acting strangely here lately."

Carson loosened his grip, ran a hand through his hair and took a deep breath. "I'm sorry. I didn't mean to hurt you. But I saw you playing football!"

Her eyes lit up, and she smiled widely. "Pretty good catch, huh? I haven't done anything like that for fifty years." She grimaced. "Maybe closer to sixty. Too long." She patted his shoulder and started again to crawl into the little car.

Again he detained her, this time with a hand on her shoulder. "Where are you going?"

She looked back at him, and he was surprised to see that she was annoyed. Grandmother never got upset.

"I told you, I'm spending the afternoon with Emily and Jeremy. Don't you remember? Are you becoming senile?"

Carson ordered himself to remain calm. Grandmother was old. He had to exercise patience in dealing with her. Likely she'd exercised enough in dealing with him when he was a child.

"I meant, where are the three of you going?"

"To the park. Don't you have some work to do or something?"

He leaned over and spoke to Emily in the driver's seat. "You'll have to excuse us. I need to talk to my grandmother. Why don't you go on without her?"

"Celia?" Emily asked, looking to the older woman for direction.

"We'll do it another time, Emily. Great toss, Jeremy." She closed the door behind her and glared at him. "That was extremely rude. I don't think I care to visit with you right now. Please take me home, or I'll call a cab."

The car puttered off down the street. Carson threw his hands into the air. "Grandmother, you're eighty-four years old. You can't go to the park and play football. What if you broke something?"

"What if I didn't?"

She marched onto the porch and opened Emily's screen door.

"Where are you going?"

"To use your phone to call a cab." She rattled the knob. "Please come unlock the door."

"That's Emily's door," he said quietly. "Come on. I'll drive you home if that's what you want." Maybe he could talk some sense into her on the way.

"I got confused about the doors because I'm so angry," she snapped. "*Not* because I'm senile."

He tried to talk to her on the drive over, but she was unresponsive. He couldn't recall when he'd seen her this upset. Certainly not in recent years. Was this another symptom of the aging process?

He walked her to the door of her unit and bent to kiss her cheek. She allowed the caress, giving him a kiss in return.

"I'm sorry I lost my temper," she said. "I know you mean well, and you've been awfully kind to me. I love you dearly, sweetheart."

"I know. I love you, too, Grandmother."

"And I know you'd do anything I asked."

He stepped back, folding his arms and studying her innocent expression. What was she up to? "As long as it didn't harm you."

"This won't. All I ask is that you stay away from Emily."

His arms dropped to his sides. "Stay away from Emily?" What on earth was she suggesting? "Other than living above her and collecting rent from her on a monthly basis, I don't imagine I'll be around her very much."

"Don't be obtuse. I saw the way you looked at her yesterday. You dropped her hand like it was on fire, but you made love to her with your eyes. And don't arch your eyebrows at me. I'm not so old I've forgotten about sex. She's a lovely girl, and you're a handsome man." She pointed a finger at him. "She's a happy, free-spirited girl who knows how to have a good time and live life to the fullest. Don't infect her with your stodginess."

Carson gave a half laugh. "I wish you didn't have so much trouble expressing yourself, Grandmother. So you think I'm stodgy because I try to get things done, because I take on some responsibility? Somebody has to do the work so the Emilys of the world can flit around and be carefree."

She patted his cheek. "You're a wonderful boy. I'm very proud of you. You know that." She unlocked her door and went in, calling over her shoulder, "Stay away from her. You could never make her happy. She needs a man who can keep up with her, who isn't afraid of new experiences." Her tone lilted as though she were taunting him, daring him. . . .

He shook his head. That made no sense. He was being too imaginative. He lifted his hands in a gesture of surrender. "Okay, okay. No problem."

He'd gladly stay away from Emily—right after he had a talk with her and got a few things straight.

Emily returned exhilarated and exhausted after spending the afternoon in the park with Jeremy.

She entered her front door and surveyed her new home with a thrill of pleasure but, as always upon entering an empty house, a burst of loneliness. Although she knew it was supposed to be healthy to enjoy being with yourself, she still preferred to have her place full of friends.

Maybe she'd get a cat. Carson had told her it would be all right.

She grabbed a chocolate-chip cookie from the kitchen, then went in to shower.

The doorbell rang just as she was drying off. Slipping on her old, blue terry-cloth robe, she went to answer it.

"Carson! Hello. Uh, come in." She stepped back, inviting him in though she wasn't sure if he was paying a social call or planning to evict her. He'd seemed pretty upset when he hauled Celia off earlier in the day.

But he didn't look angry as his gaze darted from her face to her robe and back again. In fact, his expression was downright warm—so warm she was suddenly very aware of her state of undress.

Her body responded to the heat from his green gaze with an answering glow, and for a brief instant she wondered how he'd look at her if she suddenly tossed the robe away entirely. Though the idea had a certain appeal, of course she wouldn't do it. She clutched the folds a little more tightly around her instead, her fingers gripping the fabric, a smile stealing onto her lips at the thought of how fast he'd lose his stodginess if she lost her grip.

"I'd like to talk to you about something," he said, his voice a little husky. "Maybe I could come back later, after you get dressed."

"No, no. Have a seat. I can throw on some clothes in half a minute."

She grabbed a vase, a stuffed dog and several books off one of the sofa cushions.

Carson sat...politely but tentatively on the edge of the faded floral pattern.

"Be right back!" She dashed into the bedroom and rummaged through her dresser drawers for a pair of shorts—preferably one that didn't have paint or grass stains. Adding her new, royal blue T-shirt, she checked her image in the mirror.

Wet hair and no makeup! She looked like a drowned cat.

She ran a comb through her hair, then pulled down a fringe of bangs so the image wasn't quite so stark.

As she searched in vain for her second sandal, she pulled herself to an abrupt halt. What on earth was she thinking about, trying to look good for Mr. Stuffy?

But his stare hadn't been at all stuffy a few minutes before when he'd looked at her in her robe. Her fleeting thought came back—he did have Celia's genes somewhere inside that designer shirt.

She gave her wet hair a final fluff and scowled. Was she letting desire override her good sense? Probably. She ordered herself to be cautious with this one.

Ignoring the little voice in the back of her head that whispered "cautious" was an unknown adjective in her vocabulary, she went back into the living room.

Carson still perched on the sofa, feet flat on the floor, hands clasped in his lap, looking painfully uncomfortable, and she was reminded that his mission might not be friendly.

"Can I get you something to drink? Cola? Beer?" Enough beers and he'd likely loosen up, lean back and relax.

"No, thank you."

"Have you had dinner yet?" she called over her shoulder as she went into the kitchen. "I'll just bring out a few snacks."

She gathered up tortilla chips, garlic dip, picante sauce, crackers, a jar of peanut butter, a fairly new package of chocolate-chip cookies and two cold beers, and loaded it all onto a large silver tray. Surely he wouldn't evict her while they were breaking bread together. Well, breaking tortilla chips together. It was practically the same thing.

His eyes widened slightly as she reentered the room.

"Here we go," she said, setting the tray on the coffee table in front of him. "Help yourself." Surely with that much variety, he'd find something he couldn't resist. "You might as well have the beer. It'll only go flat now that it's been opened." She sat down on the floor across the table from him, scooped up a big bite of picante sauce with one of the chips and popped it into her mouth.

"That's a very nice serving tray," he said, leaning forward to study the intricate scrollwork. "Is it a family heirloom?"

She laughed. "Probably, but not my family. I got it at a garage sale." She spread crunchy peanut butter on a cracker. "I love things with a history. Like that sofa you're sitting on. My friend Ruth's great-great..." She counted on her fingers. "Well, a bunch of greats. I forget how many. Anyway, her ancestress came to Missouri from Tennessee in a covered wagon, which doesn't hold a lot of furniture. So when they got a house built, she had that sofa sent by rail. Then through the years it got stuck up in the attic until Ruth's mother brought it down and had it recovered when Ruth and her brother were kids so they couldn't ruin her new one."

She munched on the cracker, watching Carson closely. He appeared intrigued with the story, his attention diverted. He'd picked up the can of beer and taken a sip while she'd talked. Further, his expression had loosened, and he was leaning forward, elbows on his knees, regarding her intently.

"So how did it get from Ruth's family to yours?" he asked.

"Ruth came over to see me at my old place and got tired of sitting on the kitchen-table chairs. Her mom had relegated the sofa to the attic again, and she said I could have it if I wanted it. Of course, I did. Can't you almost feel the presence of everybody who's ever sat there?"

She leaned over and laid a hand on the cushion, next to his leg.

Big mistake. All those invisible people were the least of what she could feel. Heat from his bare thigh throbbed across the scant inch separating her flesh from his. Dark hairs curled outward, almost seeming to quiver.

No "almost" about it. They were moving. She watched in fascination as his thigh muscles flexed.

Abruptly he stood, and she jerked her hand back, her elbow dipping briefly into the garlic dip. Oh, jeez! If she were cool about it, maybe she could get into the kitchen and rinse it off and maybe he wouldn't notice.

"That's fascinating," he said. "I have a drop-leaf table that belonged to my great-grandmother."

She nodded absently, trying to look casual as she got to her feet. Before she could stop him, he came around and took her elbow to help her rise.

His eyes widened in surprise. He withdrew his hand and looked at it.

"Garlic dip," she explained. Terrific! Get a sexy man in her living room, one whose thigh muscles quivered when she got close, and what did she do?

Other women might smear that man with whipped cream, but not her. She used garlic dip.

"What..." He watched, a dazed expression on his face, as she stood and lifted her arm.

"It's washable," she assured him, leading him toward the bathroom. He hesitated outside the door. "Come on," she urged, turning on the faucet and rinsing off her own arm.

Good grief. She wasn't trying to get him into the shower. Though that wasn't a bad idea. If she smeared garlic dip all over him...

He stepped in, washed his hands, and accepted the towel she handed him.

The space she'd considered large and open, cool with its yellow and green tile, suddenly seemed small and warm. Surely the heat from her shower wasn't still lingering.

She looked into Carson's ocean-bright gaze and knew that green was not necessarily a cool color. He handed her back the towel, the gesture incredibly erotic. His body filled the empty spaces, crowded impossibly close to her, yet he hadn't moved, stood a respectable distance away.

She swallowed hard, reminding herself that this was her landlord, her neighbor, Celia's grandson, a very sedate, very boring—no, at this point in time, she'd never convince herself of that last adjective.

He lifted a hand to her neck, tangled his fingers through her hair. She thought he groaned, but maybe it was her as she tilted her face up to his. In his eyes, just before he closed them, she saw astonished desire.

He was no more astonished than she, Emily mused as she drank in the sensation of his lips approaching hers, the soft warmth that sent shivers all over her body and a loud ringing in her ears the instant they touched.

They both jerked back.

Damn! That ringing wasn't from unbridled desire; it was the telephone.

Carson dropped his hand and stepped aside, allowing Emily to dart past him. He took a shuddering breath and clenched his fist.

Damn the telephone! And thank heaven for it.

This wasn't like him, totally losing control. Especially over someone like Emily who, in addition to being a klutz, wasn't even sexy in a traditional sense. She looked too fresh, too open to ever grace the pages of *Playboy* magazine. Not that she lacked any of the attributes. In addition to her long, lanky legs and pert derriere, that robe she'd had on—or almost had on— when he'd come to the door had revealed rounded, tanned breasts. She must sunbathe in the nude.

He whirled around, turned on the cold water in the sink and threw some on his face. He had to quit thinking like that. Not only did he have a business relationship with this woman, but even if he didn't, they had nothing in common. She was a hyperactive fruitcake, and he was a businessman, a politician, someone who had to preserve a respectable image. This odd attraction was strictly physical. There could never be anything between them but sex.

Ignoring the little voice that asked him if that would be so bad, he retrieved the yellow towel she'd given him for his hands and dried his face. And noticed that her towel smelled like sunshine.

Heart beating erratically, illogically, he folded and hung it carefully beside another one, probably from her shower, that she'd draped messily over the rod.

Ignoring his inclination to fold it and hang it correctly, also, he started out of the bathroom, but turned back, drawn irresistibly to bury his face in the towel she'd used to dry her body.

Sunshine and soap and spring breezes.

Nothing remotely sexy.

So why was he becoming aroused again?

He bolted from the bathroom, back to the single sofa cushion she'd cleared off for him, and slugged down half the can of beer.

From the bedroom he heard her voice, excited crystal tones. "Elaine, that's wonderful! When? Tell me all about it!"

It sounded like she might be a while. Maybe he ought to leave. After all, he'd only come down to...what had he come down for? His mind fuzzed on him, and he didn't think it had anything to do with the beer.

Oh, yes. To talk to her about his grandmother, to explain why she couldn't encourage someone in such fragile health to play football.

Emily leaned around the corner of the bedroom. "Help yourself to another beer or whatever you can find. I'll just be a minute."

Another beer. Right. That's all he needed ... more alcohol so he'd lose more of his inhibitions, his good sense.

He drummed his fingers on the sofa arm and looked around the room. It was scarcely recognizable from the time his grandmother had lived there. In spite of the difference in their ages, Emily had the same style furniture, but clutter reigned where once everything had been immaculate.

Of course, Grandmother hadn't always been so tidy. When he'd gone to visit her as a child, her house had been more relaxed than his mother's perfection. At Grandmother's, he'd been permitted to put his feet on the sofa, carry his toys to the living room, eat peanut butter and crackers though he inevitably made a mess.

He picked up a saltine, took a bite, then spread on a little peanut butter. He hadn't eaten that delicacy since he was a child. In fact, he'd never had it at home, only when he went to see his grandparents in their big old house. And Grandmother had always served crunchy style, just like Emily.

And with it, red Kool-Aid. He didn't care if it was strawberry or raspberry or cherry, so long as it was red.

"My girlfriend's getting married, and I'm going to be her maid of honor!" Emily beamed as she flopped down onto the floor across from him and handed him another beer, pulling him out of his reverie. "Now," she said, "you were telling me about your great-grandmother's table."

"I was?" A thousand years ago, maybe. Before he'd touched her and brushed her lips and found her scent in her towels.

She leaned over to take a cookie, pulling the thin material of her T-shirt taut across the rounded curves of her breasts, the peaks of her nipples.

He'd better talk to her about Grandmother immediately and get out of there.

"A drop-leaf table, you said. I have one, too." She indicated the space between two windows where a battered table held a large Tiffany-style lamp. "Of course, it isn't from my family, but my friend, Ginger, made the lamp for me."

"You need to refinish it," he said. "The table, I mean. The lamp's gorgeous." How many friends did she have, anyway?

"Oh, no. It ruins old furniture to refinish it. That would be erasing its past. Tell me about your table's past."

She spoke as though the inanimate furniture had a life of its own. "There's not much to tell. Great-grandmother gave it to Grandmother when she married. She used it, got a new one, put the old one in the attic, then passed it on to Dad when he married Mother, who also replaced it. I found it in my grandparents' attic when I was a kid and hauled it out to use as the roof of my hideout. And now, after much sanding and staining, it sits in my living room."

Her eyes shone brightly—wetly?—as she gazed up at him. Surely she wasn't crying. A small smile touched the corners of her mouth.

"That's a wonderful story," she said softly. "Can I see your table sometime?"

"Sure, I guess so." He'd never before had a woman ask to see his furniture. *Hey, babe, want to come up and see my tables?*

He cleared his throat, tried to do the same to his mind. "Emily, we need to talk about my grandmother."

"Celia's a terrific person! You're so lucky to have her." She stretched out, leaning back on her arms, her legs under the table, bare feet almost touching him.

He got his hand under control just before it reached down to capture and caress one slender foot.

"Yes. Yes, she is a terrific person."

"She'd have made a fantastic actress, but I guess in those days you had to make a choice. I'm sure she never regretted choosing a family instead. Still, it's a shame she couldn't have both."

"Yes. A shame. What! Grandmother an actress?" He sat upright on the sofa, trying to decide if Emily was making a joke of some sort.

But her gaze was puzzled, not laughing. "She never told you that was her ambition? Your grandfather met her when she was dancing on stage at the old Loew's Midland Theater."

He laughed feebly. It wasn't a very good joke.

She tilted her head to one side quizzically.

It wasn't a joke.

"Where did you hear that?"

"She told me at lunch today. You really didn't know that? Surely you just forgot."

"No. I wouldn't have forgotten something like that." He lifted the can of beer to his lips and took a desperate gulp. But then he realized what must have happened. "Just because Grandmother told you something, doesn't make it true, you know. She's getting a little senile."

This time Emily sat upright, indignantly erect. "I believe her."

The doorbell rang.

"Excuse me," she said, and rose to answer it.

He'd have to talk to Grandmother, explain that she couldn't go around saying things like that.

"Sam!"

As he watched, Emily wrapped her arms around the man's neck and gave him an enthusiastic embrace.

And suddenly a red haze enveloped the room. How could she be throwing herself at another man after the way she'd kissed him—almost kissed him—only minutes ago?

"Sam, you remember Carson, my landlord, don't you?"

"Sure. Good to see you again." Sam extended a hand, and Carson forced himself to take it, to shake it briefly before dropping it.

"Uh, am I interrupting?" Sam asked, and Carson realized his errant emotions must show on his face.

"Of course not!" Emily exclaimed, clearing another sofa cushion. "We were just having a little snack. Grab a drink and join us."

"I've got to run," Carson said, edging toward the door. "It's getting late, and we all have to work tomorrow."

"Late? It's only 9:00," she protested, and her eyes asked him to stay...or, more likely, he projected his own desires onto her.

"I have to get up really early tomorrow," he lied as she followed him to the door. "Good night."

He lay awake for a long time that night. In spite of trying not to, telling himself he wasn't doing it, he listened for sounds from below—the sound of a door closing indicating Sam had left, the sounds of lovemaking—but he finally fell asleep before he heard either.

If it were possible to hear either through the thick, old floors.

Chapter Four

The only car in the driveway the next morning was the turquoise turtle.

So what? Carson asked himself as he backed his silver Volvo out of the garage. What difference did it make if Emily had a lover? He had no desire to form a relationship with a hyperactive, noisy woman who constantly surrounded herself with other people.

At that moment she sailed out the front door and off the porch wearing a pale yellow suit, hair gleaming as it bounced in the early-morning sunshine. In her arms books and papers, obviously gathered in haste, sprouted in every direction. When she saw him, her face lit up in a wide smile.

Just a greeting since she couldn't wave, he told himself, lifting a hand. Her standard greeting, he was sure. She probably smiled that way at everyone. She was a "wide smile" kind of a person.

He pulled into the street and drove away. In his rearview mirror, he glimpsed a flash of tanned leg as she crawled into her car.

Damn! He seemed to be wearing his hormones on his sleeve here lately.

He'd been so busy trying to balance his business with his work on the city council that he hadn't taken time for a social life in several months. In fact, looking back, past the last few months, past the election, past the campaign, he was appalled at how long he'd been without female companionship.

That explained his rampant attraction to Emily. Suppressed hormones. That was all it was.

He could cure that a lot more easily and safely than risking an involvement with his tenant. He'd get tickets to the theater or a good movie for Saturday night, call Lydia, whose legs were every bit as long and tanned as Emily's, or Wanda with the flaming hair.

While he was at it, he really ought to invite Martin Wilkins and his wife to come along. Martin had thrown a lot of support his way in the election and on most of the issues since then. He was damned lucky to have such an influential man in his corner.

Yes, that's what he'd do. Combine business and pleasure.

Carson eased into his parking space with a feeling of accomplishment. He'd isolated the problem with Emily and settled on a resolution. That took care of that.

It was purely coincidental that he remained aware of her every move all week long.

Not surprisingly, most of those moves were in fast-forward mode. She dashed in from work, changed to shorts, ran out again, came home later, and charged out to her car in work clothes every morning. Just watching her exhausted him.

And drew him as surely as if a taut, invisible wire connected them.

Emily and Celia jumped up and down and cheered as Jeremy slid into home plate a fraction of a second before the ball got there.

"Your grandson?" the elderly man sitting next to Celia in the bleachers asked.

"No, just a friend."

"Wasn't that a great hit?" Emily exclaimed. "He sure had that pitcher's number!"

Jeremy was acting so cool as he accepted the congratulations and back-thumping of his teammates for his home run, but she knew he must be ecstatic. He'd come so far in the two years she'd known him. It was hard to remember what a shy, surly loner he'd been on the first day of school.

"That's my great-grandson," the older man said, pointing toward the field. "The pitcher." He slanted twinkling blue eyes around at Emily.

"Oh, dear. I'm sorry."

He laughed. "No need to apologize. It's only a game. Your friend swings a mean bat."

"Yes, he does, doesn't he? I'm Emily James." She extended a hand to shake. "And this is Celia Thayer."

"Walter Holmes." The man's grip was firm, reminiscent of Celia's.

She watched closely as he and Celia shook hands. Did he hold Celia's hand a second too long? Did Celia flush ever so slightly? Was this a relationship in the making?

Throughout the rest of the game, she kept one eye on Walter and Celia. Walter jumped up and down, clapped, cheered and booed enthusiastically. Obviously he was in good shape. His steel-rimmed glasses matched his immaculate gray hair, which he still had an adequate head of. He smiled a lot. He had several points in his favor as far as being Celia's friend.

She could hear brief snatches of their conversation. They discussed Jeremy and Aaron, Walter's great-grandson, the progress of the game...but, other than a brief, telling mention by Walter of his deceased wife, nothing personal. What was the matter with them? The game would soon be over and they'd go their separate ways.

During the seventh-inning stretch, she leaned around Celia. "I'm having some friends over for a little cookout tomorrow night. Would you like to bring your great-grandson by so he and Jeremy can make peace? Several of the boys will be there." As soon as she invited them.

"That's very nice of you. I'll ask Aaron if he's interested."

He would be, she thought. What kid would pass up hot dogs and hamburgers?

"You did say you'd be there, didn't you?" she asked Celia.

The older woman lifted one eyebrow, a faint, knowing grin touching her lips. "I wouldn't want to go back on my word. If I said I'll be there, I'll certainly be there."

"Good. Then that's settled. Here, I'll write out directions." Emily took a small notebook from her purse.

When she got home, she'd call ten or eleven of her closest friends to round out the group.

And she supposed she'd invite Carson. That would be the polite thing to do since his grandmother would be there. It would be all right, she told herself, since she would have plenty of friends surrounding her. She wouldn't have a chance to be tempted to indulge her suicidal attraction to him.

She smiled to herself as the game resumed and she passed Walter a sheet with scrawled directions. A little music, friendly people, good food, a soft spring evening—magic could happen.

To whom?

The thought thrust itself onto the forefront of her mind, but she sent it away just as quickly as it came.

To Celia and Walter, of course. Who else?

Emily gave herself a mental pat on the back for being so organized. Obviously it was true what people were always saying…that advance preparations made things go a lot smoother. Planning a party a whole day in advance was a lot easier than doing it at the last minute.

Celia had denied an interest in Walter, but she had readily agreed to go shopping with Emily tomorrow for new outfits.

Her old grill would suffice for cooking, but Emily had had no need or place for lawn furniture before she'd moved. A few friends were bringing odds and ends from their basements, and she planned to stop at any garage sales she came across the next day.

She still had a few calls to make, including Carson. She'd saved him for last, wanting to make sure everything was in place first.

And that was strange, she thought as she dialed his number. She rarely gave any consideration to having things *in place*. Jeez, she hoped his fussiness wasn't rubbing off on her.

"Hello?" His low, mellow voice came through the wires, completing the connection between them. Suddenly, inexplicably, her heart was pounding, her blood racing noisily through her ears.

She opened her mouth to speak, a feat that normally came quite easily...but this time she could only squeak.

With a dawning horror, she realized that she was overly anxious about Carson's response. His opinion mattered to her. She wanted to impress him, wanted him to like her.

Why should that be? She had lots of friends. The opinion of one man who needed to loosen his tie and his life shouldn't matter. But it did.

"Hello?" he repeated.

She tried again. "Carson." Too high. She cleared her throat. "It's me, Emily." Too low. "From downstairs." That was better. Almost normal. "I'm having some friends over for a cookout tomorrow night and, uh, I'd like you to come, too." She blurted the words before her vocal chords could betray her again.

"That's very kind of you, Emily, but I'm afraid I've already made plans."

His voice made her name sound like a poem. For a moment that was the only word she heard. Then she realized he'd refused her invitation. He wouldn't be coming. He had other plans. Her heart shrunk a little at the thought of what those other plans might be.

"Okay, well, sorry you can't make it. Maybe next time."

"I'll look forward to it. If you'd called a little earlier, I'd have been delighted to come."

Earlier? How much earlier did he want?

Mr. Conservative probably expected an engraved invitation delivered a week in advance.

And the frightening thing was, she felt crushed that he wasn't coming.

"Okay, goodbye." She dropped the receiver as though it were a snake, breaking the connection.

Shoving some odds and ends off the sofa, she sank down and buried her face in her hands. This was terrible. Having the hots for her sexy landlord was one thing—a perfectly understandable thing—but wanting him to like her, to approve of her, was quite another.

She leaned back and stared at the ceiling.

Whatever was to become of her? Next thing she knew, she'd be organizing her closet by colors and trying to balance her checkbook.

Carson measured out the gin and tonic precisely, then added three ice cubes to both glasses. Fixing a smile on his face, he carried the drinks into the living room.

That last action almost changed his expression to a scowl. He should be smiling from inside, not having to "fix" it on the outside.

From the sofa Wanda reached out a slender white hand with long red nails and accepted her drink.

"Thank you," she murmured, her voice low and throaty.

She made quite a picture against the cream-colored fabric. Dark copper curls tumbled down her back and over her shoulders, lightly brushing the blue fabric of her dress where it lay across the tops of her full breasts.

As he sat beside her, she crossed one long leg over the other, exposing a tantalizing amount of stocking-encased thigh.

Only it wasn't tantalizing to him.

He shifted, sipping his drink.

She was beautiful. She could easily grace the pages of *Playboy* magazine.

His libido was unimpressed.

She gave him a sultry look over the rim of her glass as she drank. She lowered the glass, licked the liquid from her lips. "I was beginning to think you'd fallen off the face of the earth," she said.

"When I ran for city council, I had no idea how much time it would take." He fancied he could hear happy sounds of talking and laughter from the yard below all the way through the house, through the closed balcony doors and over the noise of the air conditioner.

Of course that was absurd.

"If I know you, you're spending twice as much time and effort as anybody else."

Now he did scowl. "There's so much that has to be done. We have a desperate need to improve our inner city, to rebuild it, make it safe. Look at this neighborhood. Fifteen years ago if you saw somebody out walking after dark, you wondered what he was up to. They were dealing drugs out of this house. Now it's a peaceful neighborhood, as it ought to be."

She took his hand, her fingers cool against his. "I wasn't criticizing, Carson. I understand how important your work is."

He squeezed her hand. "Sorry." He knew he was being overly sensitive, but his grandmother's characterization of him as "stodgy" still rankled.

The doorbell rang, giving him an excuse to turn loose of her hand as he rose to answer it.

"Martin, come in. Joyce, so good to see you again. You both remember Wanda?"

As they shook hands all around, Carson prepared more drinks. "Our dinner reservations are at seven, and the movie starts at nine, so we still have a few minutes."

"Looks like they're going to be having quite a party downstairs," Martin said as Carson handed him the cool glass. "We had to park a block away. Who'd you lease to, some young, single guy?"

"A schoolteacher." Carson took a hearty gulp of his own drink. "She's just having a few friends over to a barbecue."

"Quite a myriad, I'd say, from the types of vehicles." Martin raised an eyebrow as he lifted his glass.

"Well, yes, she does attract a variety of people." And what was so wrong with that? "But they're all voters. Right?"

He watched Joyce wandering around, inspecting everything. What was she looking for? A little dust? Trying to determine the value of his furnishings?

And why was he irritated by the trait he'd observed and not minded in her before? What was going on with him?

He needed this outing. His nerves were a little frayed.

"You have such a lovely view out back," Joyce said, looking through the kitchen and out the windows in the French doors that led to the balcony. "It's a shame to waste this marvelous weather by staying inside. Can't we take our drinks out there?''

Out back? Overlooking Emily and her party? A tiny part of him tugged him in that direction, but he refused to listen. He'd planned this evening to get Emily out of his mind.

''There's a great view from the front balcony, too, and it's larger. Let's try that one.''

''On the street with all that traffic?'' She was already opening the back doors. ''And you have these darling little chairs out here.''

''Well,'' he capitulated, against his better judgment, ''shall we go sit in those 'darling little chairs'?''

After the cool of his air-conditioned rooms, the warm air was almost sensuous. The smell of charcoal lighter fluid recalled pleasant visions of steaks and ribs.

But his entire attention focused on Emily. He suspected it probably would have even if she hadn't been standing beside a roaring bonfire.

Sam stood next to her. Of course.

And what did he care who stood next to her?

''How much lighter fluid did you put on it?'' he heard Sam demand.

''Enough to get it started obviously!'' She lifted her chin defiantly. ''The charcoal got wet in the move. I thought it needed a little extra. Don't get all bent out of shape. It'll burn down.''

''I'm just glad it wasn't near the house.''

''You know I'll never again fire up the grill close to the house after what happened at your place.''

Sam clapped a hand to his forehead and groaned, and they both laughed.

Carson watched in inexplicable total fascination. She was a pyromaniac in frayed cutoffs and bare feet and his fingers tingled with wanting to touch her sun-bronzed skin, to stroke through the silky heat of her hair as it glowed in the light from the flames and the sun, to see the laughter in those golden brown eyes turn to desire as bright as the blaze before her....

Wanda touched his arm and he became aware of the voices around him.

"Could be dangerous," Martin was saying.

The fire had singed a few branches of the nearby lilac bush, but they'd grow back, Carson thought testily. He wanted to tell Martin not to get all bent out of shape.

"Neat fire!" Below them, Jeremy and a couple of other boys raced up to the conflagration.

As Emily turned toward them, her gaze lit on him. A smile started on her lips and the hand not holding the can of lighter fluid lifted...but both froze in midaction. Her gaze shifted infinitesimally to his left, to Wanda. Her eyes shadowed.

Beside him, Wanda's grip on his arm tightened. He heard the ice rattle in her glass, assumed she was taking a drink, that she felt the slight change in Emily's stare, too.

He took an involuntary step backward, but Emily had already turned away from him and was talking to Jeremy as though she hadn't noticed him.

But he knew she had. She'd seen him, and she'd seen Wanda. And that second observation had sent— he thought—*jealousy* skittering across her open, uncensored face.

He cringed inside, yet a part of him exulted that she'd been jealous, that she wanted him just as he wanted her.

"What an odd person," Wanda murmured. "She looks positively demented."

"Is that your schoolteacher tenant?" Martin asked.

"I'm afraid so."

But Martin was looking to the other side of the yard, away from Emily. "The old lady in the neon purple tunic? She looks like quite a character."

Carson looked down to see his grandmother in the inappropriate attire, holding a can of beer and having an animated conversation with a gray-haired older man.

He groaned and sat down in one of his "darling little chairs."

A horrible screeching rent the air, sending him shooting right back up.

His three guests tried to cover their ears.

Below them, Emily rushed up to the new arrival and gestured for him to turn down his boom-box.

The noise became bearable, but still the beat pulsated upward, matching the cadence of Carson's blood as it pounded past his ears. Though he couldn't tell how much of the throbbing came from desire and how much from anger. The only thing he knew for sure was that both emotions were generated by and directed at Emily.

"Perhaps we should leave a few minutes early," he suggested, taking a handkerchief from his pocket and blotting the perspiration from his brow. The temperature seemed to have risen at least ten degrees since they'd come outside.

"Good idea," Martin approved, then clapped him on the back. "I know a good lawyer if you have to evict."

"I have a good lawyer," Carson replied stiffly.

But maybe that was the answer. Get her out of his house, out of his sight, out of his mind...and his hormones.

They entered the quiet haven of his apartment, and as they walked through to the front door, Carson could feel his tense muscles begin to relax, the knot in his gut start unraveling.

But on the front porch he once again heard the music, the voices and laughter, smelled the lighter fluid, and his stomach clenched with tension...and an odd, totally inexplicable yearning to be a part of it all.

"Wait here while I get my car." He stepped off the porch, then halted abruptly. Both sides of the driveway were completely blocked.

"Let's take mine," Martin offered.

"No." He kept his voice quiet, well-modulated, quelling the shout that fought to emerge from his throat. "I'll go ask them to move their cars."

Ms. Emily James had to be dealt with. She couldn't come into his life, wreck his peace and quiet, lead his ailing grandmother astray, embarrass him in front of his friends, *and* block his Volvo.

He charged around the side yard. While one part of him observed his anger in appalled amazement, the other part held on to it, gloried in it. As long as he was angry, he was more in control than when he was lusting after her.

He shoved the gate open and looked around for her. She wasn't over by the grill any longer. Sam stood there, poking the briquettes with a long fork, assuming the role of host—as usual.

He was mad at Sam, too, though he couldn't have said why, and he shied away from trying too hard to figure it out.

He finally spotted Emily coming out the kitchen door with a foil-covered cookie sheet holding hamburger patties and wieners.

As he made his way toward her several people looked at him curiously. In his suit and tie, he didn't exactly blend with the cutoffs-and-sneakers crowd. Nevertheless, everyone smiled. One man offered him a beer. For a brief, impossible instant, he reached out, touching the cold can, considering taking it and joining the noisy, irritating, seductive insanity around him.

But sanity prevailed. He jerked his hand back and shook his head, walking rapidly away.

By the time he got to Emily, she had reached Sam's side and was tossing meat onto the grill.

"Those briquettes can't be ready yet," Carson exclaimed in horror. "You'll burn everything you put on there this early."

She looked up at him, startled. "I'm hungry," she snapped. "That means the briquettes are ready."

Sam laughed. "We've come to love blackened burgers. At least she serves great beer. Good to see you, old man. I thought you weren't going to be able to make it tonight."

Old man? Did he mean that literally? He couldn't be more than four or five years older than Sam.

"He can't make it," Emily stated firmly. "He's busy." She plopped several wieners onto the grill with what seemed to him undue vigor.

She *is* jealous, he thought exultantly, then gave himself a mental kick for such lunatic feelings.

"Your friends have got my car blocked. I can't get out, and *my* friends and I need to leave."

"Oh, dear! I'm sorry. I guess I forgot to warn them." She handed the tray to Sam. "I'll find out who the cars belong to and make them move."

She whirled away and was gone. Automatically he took a step forward, going after her, but brought himself to an abrupt halt. What would he do if he caught her?

"She'll take care of it," Sam assured him. "Did you see Celia? She's over there." He nodded in the general direction of the purple glow.

"Who's that man she's talking to? Did he come with her?"

"That's Walter. She and Emily met him at Jeremy's ball game."

Of course. He should have guessed that Emily had something to do with it. He'd be willing to bet Emily had helped her pick out that godawful outfit, too.

He charged off in the direction Emily had taken. If he could just find her, he'd put both hands around her neck, that slim, tanned neck with the smooth, baby-soft skin he remembered so vividly, and...

He pulled up short at the gate. How had his thoughts of murder gotten so far off course?

Throttle her! That's what he'd do if he found her.

He stopped searching, fled into the garage and dove inside his Volvo. With the windows rolled up, the smells and sounds of the party were muted, barely reached his overloaded senses, couldn't lure him like a manic siren song. He rubbed a hand across his forehead, realizing with a sense of inevitability that he had developed a monster headache.

Soon, though, the path behind him cleared, and he pulled out, away from the melee.

Stopping long enough to pick up Wanda, Martin and Joyce, he drove down the street, breathing a sigh of relief . . . tinged with an inexplicable feeling of regret. Was this how Ulysses had felt, lashed to the mast of his ship as he sailed away from the Sirens?

He kept his gaze focused on the road ahead, afraid to look in the rearview mirror, afraid he'd see a long-legged vision in cutoffs. He had no idea how he'd react to that, and he didn't want to find out. He wasn't lashed to his steering wheel.

Chapter Five

"What's with your landlord?" Sam asked when Emily rejoined him at the grill.

"Terminal boredom would be my best guess." Although he probably wouldn't be bored with a gorgeous redhead on his arm. She had no doubt he'd find some way to entertain himself.

"He didn't even go over to say 'hi' to his grandmother."

Emily shrugged. "Maybe he's upset about the lilac bush." When he'd first stomped up, she'd assumed that was what he'd wanted to talk to her about. But evidently the problem of singed foliage was overshadowed by his precious car's being blocked.

"Which doesn't excuse his being rude to Celia," she added.

She slid her spatula under a hamburger patty and flopped it over, giving it a vicious, flattening smack.

"Easy, kiddo. You're going to push it through the grate."

"Emily! Catch!"

She turned barely in time to snare the baseball Jeremy threw at her.

"Since that guy's gone, can we go in the front yard and throw the ball?"

"If you want to, but the food's just about ready."

Jeremy exchanged glances and shrugs with the other three boys, including Walter's great-grandson. "Okay. We'll eat first."

"Go fix your plates, then come get your meat." She indicated a weathered picnic table covered with paper plates, soft drinks, chips and side dishes contributed by her friends, many of whom cooked.

The boys charged off in that direction.

It was a good party, she decided, looking around her. Everyone was laughing, talking, drinking—Celia and Walter appeared to be enjoying themselves. She was surrounded with friends—people she cared about, people who cared about her. She should be having fun, too, in spite of the pall of gloom Carson had somehow cast over her.

"I brought your favorite chocolate cake!" someone yelled from the doorway.

"All right!" she answered enthusiastically. Of course she was going to have fun. Carson was just an irritating pebble in the smooth sand of her beach.

The last person had left and Emily was pulling on her oversize nightshirt when she heard the front door open and footsteps—Carson's footsteps—ascending the stairs. She paused, listened closely for the lighter sounds of high heels, then uttered a soft curse as she realized what she was doing.

Pulling on her robe, she grabbed a cola and took herself out to the backyard so she wouldn't be tempted to listen for creaking noises or groans from upstairs.

"That's crude," she chastised herself, unfolding the chaise lounge with a couple of vinyl strips missing. "I will not have you acting that way."

She settled the chair near the undamaged lilac bushes beside the back porch and stretched out, tucking the soft robe around her and sipping her cola.

Whatever her motivation in coming outside, the end result was a pretty good idea, she decided. The sliver of a new moon didn't dim the myriad bright stars that sprinkled the dark sky. The lilting scent of lilacs washed over her. Maybe she'd just spend the night right there. Her eyelids became heavy, and she allowed them to droop closed.

The noise of a door opening brought her fully awake and drew her attention to the balcony above. Carson came out, his profile toward her, and moved to the front rail. He wore white pajama bottoms—silk pajama bottoms, she assumed from the way the material clung to his thighs, outlining corded muscles even in the darkness. Hair that undoubtedly matched what she'd already seen on his legs created a shadow over his chest.

She swallowed hard, her mouth suddenly dry, afraid to take another drink of her cola for fear he'd notice the movement and see her. Who, she couldn't help but wonder, might be wearing the top to those pajamas?

Damn him! Just when she'd almost relaxed into sleep, he had her mind going again, speculating, conjuring up all sorts of lurid visions.

Against her will, she continued to watch, but no one joined him. He stood at the rail looking out into the night, occasionally lifting a glass to his lips.

Finally he drained the glass and heaved a sigh that drifted down to her in the still night. With a gesture of finality, he tossed the ice cubes over the side, directly into her lap.

She suppressed a shriek, but leapt to her feet and shook the ice into the grass. Had he seen her after all and done that on purpose? She glared at his bare back as it disappeared through the door.

Shivering in the night air that had become chilly, especially since she was now wet, she stomped back inside to her heated water bed. She could always use earplugs if things got too noisy upstairs.

She changed to a dry shirt and had just settled into bed when she fancied she could hear the faint murmur of voices from above.

Leaning over the side of her bed, she yanked open the drawer of her nightstand and began frantically searching for the tiny foam rubber plugs she'd bought last year when the rock band rented the apartment below hers. Among the odds and ends, she found her missing sandal, an overdue library book, a package of smashed Oreo cookies, and a hammer she'd been looking for all week.

She studied the hammer, smacking it into one palm a couple of times. She needed to hang her pictures, but it was after midnight. Perhaps she ought to wait until morning.

Peggy would say that finding the hammer at that particular moment had a meaning in the cosmos, namely that she was supposed to hang her pictures immediately. The only person she might disturb was

Carson, and she knew for a fact he wasn't asleep. And if she interrupted something, well, it served him right for tossing his ice cubes on her.

She scrambled out of bed and picked up the painting of an old barn that Paula had done for her. That would look nice on the far wall. She located a nail, poised it against the wall and smashed. It took more than a couple of blows to get the blasted thing in. Her aim had never been very good.

Settling the painting into its new home, she turned to the astrological poster Ruth had given her commemorating the fact that the two shared the same birthday. It was large, and should go above her bed.

Standing on the water bed made hammering even more erratic, but the picture would cover the marks left in the white plaster. The voices from the floor above seemed to be getting louder, so she pounded faster to cover the noise and preserve Carson's privacy.

As she stopped hammering long enough to hang the poster in place, in the silence she heard a small clicking noise—in her apartment! She turned around to see her bedroom door opening. Heart pounding, she leapt toward the intruder, hammer poised above her head.

Carson, wearing only his pajama bottoms and a wild expression, charged inside.

Emily stifled a scream, and almost threw her arm out of its socket diverting the arc of her weapon.

"What on earth are you doing?" he demanded. His hair was mussed, his eyes wide, his face flushed. It was the first time she'd ever seen him out of control.

Of course, all those symptoms weren't necessarily caused by her picture hanging.

"Did you ever hear of knocking?" she asked irritably. "How'd you get in here, anyway? I locked my door. Didn't I?" She stepped back from him and sank down on the bed, trembling, trying to catch her breath.

He threw his arms into the air and uttered a most impressive string of expletives. "I knocked, I rang the doorbell, I shouted. You were so busy trying to tear down my house, I'm not surprised you couldn't hear anything. Since I'm your landlord, I have a key for emergencies, and this certainly sounded like one."

She lifted her chin defiantly. "I was only hanging a couple of pictures." She gestured to the walls.

He ran a hand through his hair and let out a long sigh, much bigger and louder than the one on the balcony. "Do you know what time it is?"

She checked the alarm clock on her nightstand. "A little after one."

He nodded. "Did you also know that some people sleep at this hour of the night?"

"You were awake. I heard you talking."

"I was trying to sleep. I wasn't talking. I just turned on the television for some white noise."

Television? Maybe he had been alone. Surely he hadn't been watching the tube if he had company. Even he couldn't be that unimaginative. That knowledge made her unreasonably happy.

"Like I said, you were awake," she defended.

She'd been right about the hair on his chest. It formed a thick, curly mat, tapering down to vanish inside the waistband of his pajamas. She'd been right about them, too. They were definitely silk.

He hadn't even taken time to put on shoes. Bare feet protruded from the bottoms—bare, flat feet.

She started to giggle. Somehow that imperfection made him more human, more accessible.

Though she couldn't imagine how he'd ever allowed his feet to get out of line like that.

"What on earth do you find amusing about this situation?" He crossed his arms over his chest and glowered, but his voice didn't sound nearly as stern as he looked.

"I don't know. I guess I'm slaphappy." She waved a hand negligently. "Being up so late and all."

Carson didn't believe her for a minute. She didn't look the least bit tired or sleepy. Her eyes were bright, and she looked quite radiant.

He studied her as she perched on the edge of her bed wearing a nightshirt with a design of a rainbow and a castle in the clouds. Appropriate, he thought, for someone who always had her head in the clouds.

The damned shirt was big enough to accommodate the two of them but not long enough to hide her sleek legs. In spite of her ridiculous attire, she looked unbelievably sexy, and he was torn between running from the room or leaping onto the bed beside her.

He cleared his throat. "Well, if you're through decorating, I'm going back to bed to try to get a little sleep." He eyed other pictures sitting on the floor along one wall. "You are through for the night, aren't you? May I assume that nothing dire will happen to these others if they have to sit on the floor one more night?"

She twirled her hammer and cocked her head to one side impudently. "Yes, I guess so." She rose from the bed, and the patchwork quilt began to move and shift as if alive.

"What is…oh, my God, you have a water bed. You never mentioned you have a water bed."

"You didn't ask. Haven't you ever had one? They're great for your back, and they aren't any heavier per square inch than a refrigerator, so you needn't worry. Perfectly safe." She reached down and gave the covers a push.

He watched the undulations in total fascination, imagining Emily's tanned body writhing under that quilt.

He gulped and turned away, knowing the silk pajamas he wore hid nothing. "If you get an urge to work on your kitchen range, try to restrain yourself until morning," he called over his shoulder as he all but ran from the apartment—before he lost all control and leapt onto that pulsating water bed, pulling her with him.

Carson awoke the next morning at his usual hour in spite of the late night before. When he went down to get his Sunday paper, he experienced a brief thrill of disappointment that it lay neatly folded, completely intact. Their shared reading last Sunday had actually been quite pleasurable.

But Emily was probably still asleep. She'd been up as late as he. Well, almost as late. He doubted that she'd had to take a cold shower or read a couple of chapters from a travel book to get to sleep.

He took his coffee and paper out to the balcony, waved to Mrs. Johnson, and tried to settle into his routine. But he found his ears straining for sounds from the apartment below.

Which action was not, he assured himself, solely a result of his excessive production of testosterone when

Emily was around. No, his desire for her was balanced with at least an equal amount of fear. Heaven only knew what she was going to do to him next.

"Hi!"

Carson looked over his paper in the direction of the shout. Emily jogged up the street, a newspaper clutched in one hand. Her face shone with perspiration, and her tank top clung damply to her breasts. As always, she was smiling.

She turned into the yard and collapsed on her back in the grass.

He shot to his feet in alarm. She was too young to be having a heart attack. Though considering the way she lived...

He dashed downstairs.

She was definitely still breathing, her chest heaving mightily, pushing loud gasps through her open mouth.

He knelt beside her. "Are you all right?"

"I...don't think...so," she panted, wiping the sweat from her eyes.

"Shall I call an ambulance?" Her cheeks were flushed a bright, unnatural red.

She made an odd noise that sounded remotely like a laugh. "No!"

"What's wrong? What have you been doing?"

She pulled herself to a half sitting position. "Jogging."

"I didn't know you were a jogger." From the house to the car and back again, maybe.

"I wasn't." Her breathing was settling down, didn't sound quite so violent. "I thought I ought to try it." Pause to take a deep breath. "The first part was kind of nice...." She shrugged, grinned. "So I kept going farther away. Maybe I overdid it."

He scowled at her, unsure if he was relieved she was all right or angry at her for scaring him. He rose, dusting his hands. "Your paper's all crumpled," he said, turning to go back inside.

She rose shakily beside him, her grin widening. "So I'll iron it." She touched his chest gently. "There's a spot on your shirt."

Looking down, he saw a small brown stain on his blue-and-white striped shirt. He must have splashed coffee on himself when he'd set his cup down so hurriedly to check on her.

"I'm serving cola and Lucky Charms with chocolate milk if you'd care to join me for breakfast . . . as soon as I get my paper ironed."

She staggered onto the porch, pert bottom almost visible in those skimpy athletic shorts.

"I'm taking Grandmother out," he called after her. *For healthy food,* he wanted to add.

"Another time, then."

He shook his head as she disappeared inside. *Iron her newspaper.* He'd be willing to bet she didn't even own an iron. If she did, she probably used it to make grilled cheese sandwiches.

A pretty grotesque picture. So why was he smiling?

Emily heard Carson leaving just as she was finishing her second bowl of cereal. She hadn't really eaten it with chocolate milk, had only said that to rattle him.

Taking advantage of the freedom of his absence, she grabbed a cola and her newspaper and went out to the front porch. Another perfect day, she thought contentedly, leafing through the sections, feeling free to leave them scattered about. She read the comics and the magazine sections, then lay back languidly. The leaves on the huge cottonwood tree beside the driveway rustled gently, hypnotically, in the breeze.

"Yo, Emily!"

She sat upright, blinking. She must have dozed off.

"Jeremy! You're out early this morning."

He approached, repeatedly tossing a baseball from his bare hand into his glove. "Boy, you sure got a mess here."

She looked around her. The ever-present wind had blown her newspaper all over the yard, up against a tree, into the hedge and even over into the next yard.

She groaned. Since moving in, she'd seemed to develop a talent for doing things that would irritate Carson—deliberately or accidentally.

"Carson won't be happy with this. Help me pick it up, okay?"

"Sure, if you'll play catch with me."

"You got it, kiddo."

They gathered up the wrinkled sheets and carried them inside to the trash can.

But Jeremy seemed in no real hurry to get to their game. He followed her dispiritedly from room to room, a sure sign his world was more disturbed than usual.

"Want some milk?" she asked.

"Nah."

"Oh, all right. Twist my arm. Go ahead." She extended one hand toward him.

He took it, smiling as he made a gentle turning gesture.

"Very well," she agreed with a mock sigh. "You can have the hard stuff." Remembering how often as a child she'd yearned for sodas and been given something "good for you" instead, she offered him a cola.

"Thank you," he said formally, accepting the red can. "You never drink milk. You drink all the sodas you want."

"That's because I don't intend to grow any more, but we certainly hope you will. Otherwise, when you're a famous surgeon, you'll have to stand on a stool to reach the operating table. That's not likely to inspire confidence in your patients. Come on. Grab a chair, and let's go outside. I'll even join you in another cola so you won't have to drink alone."

She pulled her chair close to the porch rail and put her feet on it. He did the same.

"I went jogging this morning," she told him. He was being unusually quiet.

"Oh, yeah? How'd you do?"

"Okay, I guess, but it didn't make my list of things I'd do if I only had one day to live."

That got a giggle out of him.

"So how'd your morning go?" she asked.

"Okay, I guess. Mom hadn't got home yet when I left."

"Oh. Bummer." She studied her soda can, reminding herself to minimize the situation for his benefit. He looked so small and helpless sitting there. "Did you get some breakfast? Do you want some fruit or oatmeal?"

"How come you're always trying to push that healthy junk on me?" he complained.

"Because it's good for you." She threw her arms into the air. "Okay. I got sardines in mustard sauce."

"I had a peanut butter sandwich, but I guess I could eat some sardines."

"Save some of your soda to wash them down," she warned as she went inside. "You can't have another until afternoon."

"Yeah, yeah, yeah."

She returned with the fish, crackers, a roll of paper towels and two forks. "Here," she said, offering him the unopened can.

"Cool!" He took it, inserted the key, and painstakingly, happily, rolled back the lid. He plopped a yellow-coated sardine on a cracker and munched. Emily followed suit.

"I guess Mom really likes this Fred guy," he mumbled.

"Don't talk with your mouth full," she mumbled back, and he started to laugh, covering his mouth with one hand. "And whatever else you do, don't spit crackers and sardines on Carson Thayer's immaculate porch."

He laughed so hard, he almost choked. She thumped him on the back a couple of times and encouraged him to take a drink of cola.

He finally settled back and wiped the tears from his eyes. "He's a grouch, isn't he?"

"He, who?"

"You know who. The guy who lives upstairs."

"Nah, not really. He's just kind of different from you and me."

"And everybody else in the world."

That could very well be, she thought. "Tell me about Fred. So you think your Mom likes him. Do you?"

He shrugged, picked up a sardine by its tail, tilted his head back and dropped it into his mouth. "He's okay, I guess. He's always giving me orders and being nasty when Mom's in the other room, then when she comes back, he smiles real big at me, says something dumb and tries to pretend I'm not there. I told Mom, but she got mad and said I was jealous.''

Emily munched on a cracker, marshaling her thoughts. Jeremy probably was jealous, but with good reason, she suspected.

"We're not going to make friends with everybody we meet. Like my landlord. You just have to hang on to the people who love you and ignore the rest. And you're a very lucky boy. You have scads of people who love you."

"Oh, yeah?" He deliberately threw the can of sardines onto the porch, spilling yellow goo. His expression had turned surly. "Well, if Mom loves me so much, why does she spend so much time with Fred?"

"You don't spend all your time with her, either." Though he'd probably spend a lot more if he could. "Remember what I told you. You can love a lot of people. Much as your Mom loves you, she needs others in her life just like you do." She reached over and took his small hand. "And like I do. I sure am glad I have you."

Some of the clouds lifted from his face—as many as she could reasonably expect under the circumstances.

"Can I play with your computer?" he asked.

"After you clean up the mess."

"Yeah, yeah, yeah," he grumbled, but he scrambled out of the chair and bent to the task.

The shriek of screaming tires sounded from the street. Emily looked up to see Carson's silver Volvo turn into the driveway on two wheels. She blinked, squinting against the sun to see who was driving. It must be Celia; Carson would never drive like that.

But Carson hunched over the wheel, bringing the vehicle to a screeching halt in the middle of the driveway, making no effort to put it in the garage.

She rose slowly to her feet and clutched the porch column. What could possibly cause him to act so totally out of character?

Please, God, nothing had happened to Celia.

He threw his car door open, jumped out, and slammed it behind him. She was relieved to see his brow dark with anger. It wasn't Celia.

A bird from the tree beside the driveway left a deposit on the shiny surface of his car, but Carson ignored it.

Boy, this was the granddaddy of tempers.

He strode over to the porch and glared up at her then down at Jeremy.

The boy didn't need any more trouble this morning, she decided. "I, uh, dropped some sardines," she said quickly. "Don't worry. We'll get it all cleaned up."

"Could I talk to you? Inside?" He clenched his jaw, jerking his head toward the door.

Her mind raced. He'd already been angry when he drove up, so it couldn't be about the spilled mustard sauce. What could have happened to make him mad at her when she hadn't even been present? That was a pretty good feat, even for her.

At least he wasn't going to explode in front of Jeremy.

"Sure," she said. "Come on in. You know the way. Back in a minute, Jeremy."

"I made this mess," Jeremy blurted, rising shakily to his feet and confronting Carson, his ten-year-old jaw thrust out. "Leave Emily alone."

To his credit, Carson smiled at the boy, though it was a pretty tense gesture. "Go ahead with your cleaning. We'll be finished with our discussion in a couple of minutes, and you can have her back."

"It's all right," Emily assured him. She opened the door and preceded Carson inside.

Hearing the door close behind them, she turned to face him.

He ran a distracted hand through his hair, looking more frustrated now than angry.

"Did you know Celia has a date to go dancing tonight?" he asked quietly.

"With Walter? All *right!*" So what, she wondered, was the problem? Was Walter the wrong religion or something? Surely even Carson couldn't be that scrunched up.

She dumped some books out of a Victorian-era chair, faded from some shade of pink to a soft mauve, and sat down. Her legs felt weak . . . a residual effect of the run, she told herself.

"Grandmother is eighty-four years old."

So that was it. "Okay, I admit I didn't check his driver's license. Is he too young? Too old?" What difference did a few years make?

He loomed over her, arms akimbo, fists on his hips. "Don't you think eighty-four is a little old to be going dancing?"

"Oh, good grief! No, I think dead is too old to go dancing, and I think too old to go dancing is dead." She paused briefly, then let her temper possess her tongue. "Haven't been dancing yourself in a long time, have you?"

She jumped as he smashed his fist onto one of the chair arms. "Spare me your hedonistic philosophy! If you really want to be a friend to my grandmother, take her to play bingo or bridge. If you care about her, how will you feel if she has a heart attack and falls dead on the dance floor because of your machinations?''

Emily cringed back from his anger. "If anything happens to Celia, of course I'll be devastated. But we can't live our lives based on what might happen. You could get killed crossing the street! Does that mean you'll never cross the street again?''

He thrust away from the chair, from her. "That's just exactly the kind of response I expected from you!'' He pointed a finger at her. "I'm warning you, stay away from my grandmother. I'm trying to take the best care of her I can, and you're not included in that concept.''

She leapt to her feet, shoving his finger aside. "Don't point at me. And don't treat Celia like a child. She has a mind. She can make her own decisions, and whether or not I stay away from her is up to her, not you.''

His wrath boiled barely beneath the surface, mottling his skin and blazing from his eyes. She braced herself for the next assault, but he spun on his heel and stomped out, closing the door quietly behind him. For some reason, that seemed the unkindest cut of all.

Chapter Six

When Emily thought about it, her argument with Carson bothered her a lot. So she tried not to think about it.

As always, her life was busy with school and friends, but it was difficult to ignore someone who lived overhead. Her senses seemed to be unusually acute so that she heard and recognized the sound of his car when he drove in late one night, caught a faint whiff of woodsy cologne as he passed her open door on the porch, saw his furrowed brow in the dimness of the streetlight.

Every creak and groan of the old house took on a significance. Was he walking through the kitchen at 2:00 a.m.? Skipping rope in the dining room shortly after midnight? Playing hopscotch in the basement just before dawn?

She bought a new set of earplugs and made every effort to keep him out of her world.

Friday morning she grabbed a cola from the refrigerator and a packet of strawberry Pop-Tarts from the pantry and started to dash out to her car. But as she passed the sink, she heard a dripping sound. Looking down, she saw a trickle emerging, forming a small but growing puddle on the white tile of the floor.

Damn! Just what she needed.

Squatting over the puddle, she peered under the sink. A wet pipe revealed the source of the leak but she could see no way to turn off the water. She stood, popped the top on her soft drink and took a deep, fortifying gulp.

Her landlord had to be notified.

But he'd already left. She'd heard his car going down the driveway several minutes ago.

So she'd have to phone his office. With any luck, maybe he wouldn't have arrived yet, and she could leave a message. Locating his business card in her handbag, she found the phone in the living room and dialed, carrying the instrument around with her as she paced the length of the cord and back.

This time, luck was with her. An authoritative female voice answered. "He hasn't come in yet. May I have him return your call?"

"No, he can't call me. I'll be in class. This is Emily James, his tenant. Just tell him there's a leak in my kitchen, and I don't know how to turn off the water."

"I'll be happy to give him the message, but we don't expect him until this afternoon."

Emily flopped onto the sofa. "That's just great. Well, I'll put a pan under the drip and hope it doesn't get any worse. Tell him to come over and fix it as soon as he can. I won't be here, but he has a key."

She went back into the kitchen and surveyed the widening pool. It would serve him right if the pipe burst and flooded the whole house.

No, it wouldn't, she admitted to herself with a sigh. He was completely wrong in his treatment of his grandmother and of her, but he was sincere. He was doing what he genuinely, if misguidedly, thought was right for her. What chance did he have, after all, being raised by a mother who played bridge and kept her house clean?

She set a pan under the problem pipe, cleaned up the puddle with an old towel, took up her breakfast, purse and books and prepared to leave.

But what if he didn't get there until late, and the pan ran over? What if the leak got worse?

She set her load down again. She'd just have to be a few minutes late for class. Locating a flashlight, she took a closer look.

Maybe she could wrap something around the pipe...like aluminum foil or plastic wrap or cellophane tape.... No, that wouldn't work. What she needed was a way to divert the water. She had the hose they'd used to fill the water bed. If she could somehow make it stay in place where the water was dripping and stick the other end in the sink...maybe if she took chewing gum to fill in the space then added cellophane tape.

The result looked decidedly strange and probably wouldn't last long, but maybe it would be long enough.

As added insurance she threw several old towels on the floor, then finally left for school feeling pleased with her actions. In spite of her differences with Carson, she'd done everything she could to protect his property.

When Carson got the message that Emily's plumbing was broken, he immediately wondered what she'd done to break it. How was he ever going to survive the one-year lease with a two-year option they'd signed?

Yet a maverick impulse he'd thought he had safely tucked away kept smiling inanely at the idea of going into Emily's home, being among her possessions— maybe seeing her. With an appeal to his logic, he resolutely sent that illogical impulse back where it belonged.

It was already three in the afternoon by the time he arrived, so he fully expected to find the entire house flooded by the time he got there. But the towels in front of the sink were dry. A close inspection revealed the most ridiculous makeshift arrangement he'd ever seen.

But he had to give her credit. The damn thing was working. An involuntary smile crept over his face as he imagined her working diligently to construct the arrangement. He had to admire her creativity. Anyone else would have put a pan under the leak and run the risk of water spilling over. Not Emily.

Greatly relieved that the floor wasn't ruined, he headed for the hardware store to get the necessary supplies. The task looked relatively simple, and if he hurried, maybe he could be in and out before Emily came home. The fact that he *wanted* to see her, fantasized about her walking through the front door and . . . well, that made it all the more imperative that he be gone before she got there.

After their heated encounter on Sunday afternoon, he'd tried to avoid her. Not that it took much effort since she was always running one place or another or entertaining friends. He'd seen Sam's car parked behind hers on Tuesday evening and had deliberately stayed away until late, though he wasn't quite sure why. He wasn't angry at Sam, just at Emily.

He arrived back with the supplies and was just finishing the job when he heard the turquoise turtle pull up. Running steps crossed the porch. Didn't she know how to walk?

Once inside, she slowed down, but not to a reasonable pace.

"Oh, good, you got here before it flooded."

He kept working, and didn't look out at her. "You did a pretty good job of diverting the water," he grudgingly admitted.

"Oh, it worked? Thank goodness."

Then he had to decide whether to ask for her help or slide out from under the sink knowing his head would be in the general vicinity of her knees, her tanned knees attached to her tanned calves and thighs. "Would you hand me that other wrench?" he asked, choosing the lesser evil.

"Sure. Here."

He stretched out his hand, and she laid the tool into his palm. "Thank you," he said.

And then the job was finished, and he had no choice, short of spending the night there, but to slide out and ogle her legs while trying to keep his libido in check.

He needn't have worried. The skirt of her pleated ivory dress came almost to her ankles. What leg he could see was sheathed in ivory nylon, her bronze feet hidden in ivory heels.

He rose slowly, unable to take his gaze off her. At the throat of her silk dress she wore a cameo pin. Her hair was tucked behind her ears, and makeup accentuated her shining eyes. She looked beautiful and sophisticated.

Impossible.

Yet even in the demure clothing, she exuded sensuality. The soft fabric slid over her breasts, down her hips, around her legs, hiding the tanned lusciousness he knew lay within.

His lascivious thoughts must have shown on his face because she blushed and moved away.

"Would you like a cold drink?" She opened the refrigerator and stared inside.

"No. Thanks." He dusted off his hands. "Well, that should take care of the leak. Let me know if you have any more trouble."

She closed the refrigerator and spun around toward him, her expression uncertain, almost shy.

Impossible.

Nevertheless, it did him in. "I'm sorry," he started to say, but she began to speak at the same time. They both halted, laughing nervously.

"Go ahead," he urged. "You first."

Not surprisingly, the phone rang.

"Excuse me," she said, and went to answer it. He could tell from her tone, without even listening to the words, that the caller was one of her friends. She probably never got calls from salesmen; they wouldn't be able to get through.

He picked up the towels from the floor and threw them into the sink.

He ought to go on home. He'd done the job he'd come to do.

But he wanted to apologize. He couldn't get her odd expression out of his mind, couldn't rid himself of the nagging notion that he'd hurt her feelings. Even though he had every right to complain about the way she'd led his grandmother astray, maybe he'd been a little brusque with her.

In a few minutes she returned, hands clasped in front of her. "I'm sorry about Sunday afternoon," she said softly.

His eyebrows rose in surprise.

"Not about getting your grandmother and Walter together," she added hastily, her chin tilting stubbornly upward. "Only about fighting with you."

"Emily, I—"

The damn phone went off again.

He rubbed a hand over his chin in frustration. It was just as well he had no intention of ever acting on his hormonal impulses because there'd never be an opportunity.

Leaning against the sink, he prepared to wait. He couldn't leave now, not after she'd apologized and he hadn't. In a few minutes she came back, this time minus her shoes.

"Can we go somewhere quiet and talk?" he asked impatiently. "Somewhere without a phone?" *Or the possibility that a carload of friends would show up at the door at any minute.*

"Okay. Where?"

"We could grab a burger at that new place down the street." As soon as the words escaped his lips, he looked around for the ventriloquist in the room. Had he just asked his mad tenant for a date?

No, he assured himself. He was simply trying to find a place where they could talk uninterrupted. A burger in a public place.

At least he hadn't asked her to go up to his apartment.

"Sure. Give me five minutes to throw on a pair of blue jeans." She was already heading for the bedroom.

Only after she had answered did he realize how much he'd wanted her to say yes, how disappointed he'd have been if she'd refused.

He almost called after her, asked her not to change, to let him savor looking at her a little longer in that demure/sexy outfit.

Instead he clapped his palms together. "Great. I could use a shower myself after that repair work." *Or maybe a tub bath with ice cubes instead of soap.* "Meet you on the porch in thirty minutes."

He could hear Emily's phone ringing again before the door closed behind him.

Emily dashed into the living room wearing only her slip and stockings and grabbed the phone.

"Hello?" she greeted, suppressing an unheard-of irritation at the instrument. She loved to get phone calls, verbal visits, but this afternoon the timing seemed less than desirable.

"Emily, this is Celia."

Immediately her annoyance vanished—as it had the previous two times that afternoon the minute she'd heard a friendly voice. "Tell me everything! Did you have a wonderful time?"

"I did. We danced until midnight, then drove around with the sunroof open so we could look at the stars, and we stopped at a park and stole some flowers.'' She said the last part breathlessly, excitedly.

Emily laughed. ''I can see it now. The phone rings in the middle of the night, and you say, 'Emily, I only have one call. I'm in the slammer for the sake of six irises.' ''

''And it would be well worth it.''

''That's terrific. I'm so glad. When are you seeing him again?''

''We have a flexible dinner engagement sometime this week, but for sure we're going to do something on Saturday. Which brings me to the purpose of this call. Walter thinks it would be fun for the three of us and maybe Sam to take Aaron and Jeremy to Worlds of Fun.''

''The amusement park? That's a great idea. I'll check with Sam and Jeremy and let you know tomorrow. I need to run right now. I'm getting ready to go to dinner with your grandson.''

''Oh?'' The tiny syllable came across the wire pregnant with meaning. Emily just couldn't quite figure out what meaning, whether Celia was pleased or upset. Probably upset since she'd already warned her that Carson was beyond redemption.

''Just to talk,'' she hurried to reassure her. ''It's not like a date or anything. Strictly landlord/tenant business.''

''Carson's a wonderful man, but no one could ever get him to Worlds of Fun.''

Reluctantly Emily had to agree with that. He probably wouldn't approve of his grandmother going to Worlds of Fun, either.

But he hadn't been appointed Celia's guardian, and until that time, it was really none of his business, she reasoned. Nevertheless she thought she'd keep the outing to herself. No point in rocking the already-floundering boat.

Emily studied the overhead menu. "I'll have a burger with chili, cheese, bacon, mustard, pickles..." She hesitated over the onion. Standing beside Carson, she was finding it hard to ignore the sense of maleness emanating from him, to keep her mind from conjuring up all sorts of unrealistic visions.

Get the onions, she ordered herself sternly. *You're not going to kiss him. It's not like this is a date.* "Fries and a cola," she finished.

Well, onions could be lethal even if you were just talking to someone.

"Regular burger and a diet cola," Carson told the man behind the counter.

Of course he'd order something mundane. But the thought was only an observation, not really a criticism. Might as well criticize him for having brown hair.

They collected their food on red plastic trays and Emily led the way to a red vinyl booth near a window.

He took the seat across from her, arranged his food, cleared his throat and sat up straight. She hesitated while adding massive amounts of salt to her food. Obviously he was getting ready to say something important. Probably something she wouldn't like.

"I want to apologize, also," he said formally. "For losing my temper." Before the last word had traveled across the table to her ears, he lifted his burger to his mouth and took a big bite... biting off the sentiment, keeping it impersonal, limited to an apology for incorrect behavior, not an admission that he was wrong.

She dumped catsup on her fries. "Apology accepted." That was fair enough, she decided. She hadn't admitted she was wrong, either, nor did she have any intention of changing her behavior.

They ate in silence for a few minutes. Carson finished his burger, leaving his white plate completely free of crumbs.

Naturally.

"Have some fries," she offered, shoving her own plate with crumbs, catsup and thick golden potato strips toward him. "They're very good."

Maybe he'd drop catsup on that perfect blue knit shirt that hugged his perfect pecs. He had left the top button open—or, more likely, it opened when he wasn't looking; she couldn't imagine his being deliberately casual—allowing a few dark hairs to escape and tempt her fingers.

He shook his head in response to her offer. "No, thanks." He leaned back and looked out the window beside them. "That's another restaurant going in across the street." He nodded in the direction of the ongoing construction.

"Oh, yeah? What kind?"

"Italian. It should be fairly upscale." He cupped his hands around his glass and turned it slowly back and forth. "That used to be an old service station turned into an adult bookstore."

She munched on a fry and nodded. "I think it's great that so many cities are redeveloping their older areas."

"So do I," he agreed. "It's really wasteful to let these old buildings get run-down, allow the criminal element to come in and scare away the decent people."

He absentmindedly picked up a fry from her plate and popped it into his mouth. She was pretty sure he didn't even realize what he was doing, but somehow the action was amazingly sensuous, as though his eating from her plate created a physical contact between them.

"I love the old buildings," she said quickly, not wanting him to have time to reflect on his spontaneous action and go all scrunched up on her again. "I always feel like a little bit of everyone who ever lived there still remains. A new house feels really lonely, but an old one always seems to have company just waiting in the next room."

The corners of his mouth lifted in a half smile. "I don't know about that, but the construction sure beats this new stuff. We don't even grow trees big enough to produce some of the lumber used in these old places, much less have the time to craft it as well." He ate another fry from her plate. A thrill darted down her spine as she again felt the connection, the touch that wasn't a touch.

She cleared her throat and refocused her out-of-control thoughts. "This building isn't new, is it? What did it used to be?"

"My company did the renovation," he said, the quiet pride in his voice evident. "This was a neighborhood grocery store when I was a boy. It was a little weathered even in those days. An elderly couple, Mr. and Mrs. Baker, ran the place. Grandmother knew them, and she used to bring me over here sometimes. I loved it because I always got candy or ice cream." His smile widened. "Or both. And we kept it a secret from Mother."

Emily refrained from expressing her first thought, namely that it was hard to imagine him as a child who relished forbidden sweets. Actually, when he smiled like that, it wasn't so difficult after all.

"So Celia's lived around here before?" She spoke quietly, afraid to disturb the faraway look in his eyes, break the trance he seemed to be in.

"Just a couple of blocks over. She and Grandfather had a big house they bought when my father was born. People in those days had a lot of children, so they were planning ahead." He shook the crushed ice in his glass, raised it to his lips and drained the last few drops of pale liquid.

"When did she move into the duplex with you?"

"After Grandfather died, the house was just too much for her. I was ready to buy my own place, and I thought if she lived downstairs, I could help take care of her." He scowled, and she could see his spirit returning to the present.

"I'd love to see the house where she lived," she said hastily, wanting to keep him in this agreeable state of mind as long as possible. "Does anybody live there now?"

His scowl deepened. "Grandmother sold it to an investor, and he chopped it up into apartments."

"Oh. That's too bad. Where is it?"

"Why do you want to know that?"

"Because I want to go see it."

"Why?"

"Because it's part of you and of Celia. Because I love old houses, especially if I know some of their history." She finished her drink and gathered up her handbag. She'd find out the address from Celia. Maybe they'd go see it together.

He stood. "If you want to see the place, let's go before it gets dark."

She looked up in surprise at his words. "I'm ready," she said.

They drove along the tree-lined streets filled with the ghosts of beautiful women sweeping down the steps in long dresses to join gallant gentlemen holding carriage doors for them, and of children playing hide-and-seek and kick-the-can when traffic wasn't a threat.

Emily elected to keep her fanciful thoughts to herself. Carson would probably tell her there were no such things as ghosts.

He pulled up in front of a large, two-story white house with a stained-glass window in the attic and an L-shaped porch that wrapped around the front and one side. Fish-scale shingles decorated the second floor, and large windows, some floor-to-ceiling, dominated the entire structure.

"It's gorgeous!" she exclaimed.

"It needs paint badly."

"It has so much personality."

"It probably has termites."

She pushed open the car door. "Let's go up on the porch and sit in that swing."

"You can't do that," he protested. "People live there."

"But you said they're in apartments. How will they know we're not visiting somebody?" she called over her shoulder from halfway down the walk.

As she stepped onto the porch, she could almost feel the joy and sorrow and love and fear from all the lives of all the people, past and present. She sank into the creaky swing and gave a push.

Carson, apparently in pain, judging by the expression on his face, joined her and stilled the motion of the swing.

He perched uneasily on the edge of the slatted seat just as he'd perched on her sofa that Sunday night after she'd moved in. Nevertheless he was sitting with her, and for a fleeting, crazy moment, she felt a sensation of belonging, that they were together, connected to each other and to the old home. She had to resist an impulse to edge closer, to feel his body against hers, complete the connection, dive headfirst into the nostalgic, inviting cloud of unreality.

"Did you sit here when you were a little boy?" she asked instead.

"Sometimes." His gaze stroked her face and she wondered if he had somehow drifted into her fantasy. Nah. Not him. She was being fanciful again. "I was usually too busy running around," he continued, "playing baseball or being a cop or a robber or a vampire."

She looked at him in amazement. "A vampire?"

"Or a werewolf or zombie or whatever monster was on the most recent midnight horror movie. I didn't watch things like that at home so I guess I went overboard when I came here to visit."

"You had good times with your grandparents," she observed quietly.

He relaxed back into the swing and gave it a gentle push, his eyes focused somewhere in the distance—or the past. "Grandmother was super. She let me stay up late, scream and laugh—make all the noise I wanted, play in the dirt, eat cake and ice cream."

As she watched, the tension left his face and she could see the little boy he'd been, released from his structured home life, playing happily on the porch they now sat on, in the yard they'd walked across.

"What about your grandparents?" he asked. "Did they have a big old house like this? Is that why you're so fascinated?"

The question was only fair, she thought. He'd shared his childhood with her; she should do the same with him. Though her story would probably break the cozy spell that surrounded them.

"My father's parents died before I was born, and mother's were in the same car as she and daddy when some drunk smashed into them, killing everybody. I was six at the time. I grew up in foster homes—some new, some old. I liked the old best. Sort of like borrowing someone else's history for a while."

She felt she'd told her story as succinctly and matter-of-factly as possible, but still he stopped the swing and looked at her, his eyes filled with sympathy— something she didn't want anyone to feel for her.

"That must have been rough," he said quietly.

She shrugged. "It's a long time in the past. I have a happy life now, with lots of friends and a home with a history I can borrow." His questions made her uncomfortable. She'd answered them for other people a hundred times, but Carson's gaze seemed to probe more deeply than his words, into sensitive areas she didn't want exposed.

"What was your apartment like before you moved?"

She liked that question better. It was more impersonal. "Old but small and on the third floor. Now I have lots more room for my friends to come visit, plus a yard."

He grinned. "A yard with some nice lilac bushes if you can refrain from burning them down."

She laughed, and they swung back and forth in companionable silence for a few minutes.

"Are you about ready to go?" he finally asked. "I can just see the headlines—City Councilman Arrested For Trespassing."

She stood and grinned down at him. "Oh, I don't think a city councilman trespassing would make the headlines. Maybe a short paragraph on page seven."

His answering smile was faint, but she thought she could detect its existence. Try as he might, he hadn't made a complete journey back to the present from the little boy who loved to visit his grandmother.

They walked back to the car and she had to fight the continuing feeling of a connection between them. This vulnerable, human side of him drew her, made her want to forget the other side that, she kept reminding herself, could reappear at any minute.

As they pulled away from the curb, she took one last look at the old house.

"Did Celia and your grandfather sit out on the porch on evenings like this?"

"Sometimes."

She could see the couple sitting there—young, then growing older, together. Greedily she clasped the borrowed memory.

"Did you play in that park?" she asked, pointing down a side street.

"If I say yes, does that mean we have to go there?" he grumbled.

She laughed, especially since he was already turning the car in that direction. He really was acting awfully human tonight. Had there been something besides diet cola in his drink at the restaurant?

The small neighborhood park was empty except for a few boys tossing around a ball at one end. The playground equipment was free. But challenging him to a race on the swings might be pushing his humanness.

She got out of the car and walked around sedately.

"Dandelions!" he said in disgust, looking over the green and yellow expanse. "They're not taking very good care of the grounds."

She reached down and picked one, holding it up for his examination. "They're flowers. Special flowers that don't have to be cultivated or fertilized or pampered."

His eyes held a puzzled, gentle expression as they flicked from the blossom to her face.

"I suppose you call that a flower, too?" he asked, looking away from her, indicating a seeded dandelion at her feet.

"Yes." She plucked the gauzy ball, also, and held it up, blowing on it to show him the plant's ultimate beauty. Unfortunately, Carson moved and the feathery seeds floated straight into his face and hair.

He sputtered, wiping a hand across his mouth.

Well, that ought to take care of any remnants of humanness.

"They're not poison," she murmured, reaching up to disengage a couple from his hair. "Anyway, you'd look very attractive with dandelions sprouting from your head." He looked pretty damned attractive with plain, ordinary hair sprouting from his head. But she didn't tell him that.

"Ouch!" He jerked away. "That's not a seed," he protested.

"Oh, sorry."

He grabbed her wrist as she lowered her hand, and for a minute she thought he was going to try to reclaim the hair she'd pulled. But he just held her, his fingers warm against her flesh, his eyes a deep, burning jade in the encroaching twilight. For a crazy instant she was glad she'd gotten her burger without onions. It seemed as if he was moving closer to her. She could almost feel his lips on hers.

Then he turned abruptly away. "We'd better be going. It's getting dark."

"Yes, it is," she agreed. It did indeed seem darker when he turned away from her.

They started back toward the car. The boys had left, gone home to supper, probably, and they were alone.

"Look! A lightning bug!" She stretched out her hands and caught the insect between her cupped palms.

"Firefly," he corrected.

"Whatever." She lifted a thumb and peered into her hands at the creature magically blinking its tail. "Look," she offered, then regretted her impulse. If things went the way they'd been going, she'd probably somehow manage to set him on fire with the lightning bug.

He gave her an odd smile, then bent to peek inside, cupping her hands gently with his. When he finally backed away, she opened her hands and the insect lifted its wings and flew away, winking a path across the park.

Carson stared after it, tracking its progress for several seconds, then he turned back to her. Without a word, he moved toward her, his eyes full of surprised wonder, and took her face in his hands, holding it as gently as she'd held the lightning bug.

His lips descended to hers, touched tentatively, moved away, then came back more certain this time. Leisurely, expertly, his mouth explored hers. He tasted of catsup and fries and dandelions and baseball games in the park, and a volcano exploded where his lips touched hers, sending molten lava coursing through her veins.

Even as her mind told her how insane were her actions, she slid her arms around his broad back and pressed her body against his. She'd never seen any particular benefits in being sane, anyway.

He moved one hand down her back, pulling her closer, and the other slid through her hair, holding her head as though she might try to get away from him. She'd been right about one thing; that lightning bug had started one heck of a fire.

Then he took his mouth from hers and gazed at her from half-closed eyes. "We'd better go home," he whispered huskily, breathlessly.

She nodded, didn't ask to whose home. Her body was impartial in that respect, and she'd completely lost her mind, so it didn't matter.

"I know," she said softly. "You can just see the headlines."

"A small paragraph on page seven."

Laughing, they walked slowly across the grass, side by side, Carson's arm around her waist. She stopped to pick up a maple seed, toss it into the air and watch it whirl crazily until it reached the ground. She looked at him to be sure he was sharing the moment with her. He retrieved the seed and repeated her action, watching the whirligig with a fascinated expression. When it reached the ground, he smiled at her and tightened his arm around her.

At the car, he held her door open for her.

Another vehicle pulled up beside them, and a woman leaned out. "Emily James! I haven't seen you in forever."

"Cheryal!" For a moment she stood suspended, then took the few steps to the other car. "How on earth are you? Did you finish law school yet?"

"I did. Here's my new card. Hey, you gonna be home in about an hour? I'll bring over a bottle of champagne and we'll celebrate. I have so many things to tell you!"

Emily hesitated, wanting to be with Carson, to see what might happen between them. "Well..."

"Great. I'll see you in an hour."

"I've moved," Emily mumbled in a weak protest.

"I'll find you. What's your new address?"

Feeling trapped but unwilling to reject her friend, Emily told her.

Carson was waiting in his car when she got back, and she could tell the atmosphere had changed.

"Cheryal's a really neat person," she said. "She was a legal secretary for years, then she started law school when she was thirty."

"And she's coming over in an hour." His voice wasn't husky anymore, nor was he laughing.

Emily cringed. "I'm sorry. She's my friend. That means a lot to me."

He nodded curtly. "I've noticed."

He let her out beside their front porch and went on to put the car in the garage. She waited for him to come back, though she thought he didn't expect her to.

"Thank you for dinner and sharing Celia's house and your park with me." *And for kissing me and setting my body on fire and for then showing me immediately that I can't get involved with you in spite of that.* Celia was right, but not just because Carson was boring. She'd never be able to think of him as boring again, not after that kiss, not after he'd made her feel like that maple seed, whirling and spinning through the air.

But he'd never accept her friends—or understand her need for them.

Chapter Seven

Carson settled on his balcony with his Saturday morning coffee and newspaper. A few clouds dotted the blue prairie sky, remarkably similar to the condition of his head at the moment. He hadn't spoken to Emily since that mind-shattering, body-rousing, insane kiss they'd shared.

That is, he hadn't spoken to her in person. He'd rehearsed in his mind a thousand different things he ought to say to her.

Emily, I'm sorry I kissed you.

No, not sorry. If he were sorry, he wouldn't keep reliving it in his mind.

Emily, I shouldn't have kissed you. You're beautiful and desirable, and, boy, do I ever desire you.

No, delete that last part.

We have nothing in common. You like noise and need lots of people around all the time. I like privacy and quiet. I'm a public figure. I lead a sedate life. You do crazy, frivolous, impulsive things. You drive me crazy, set my nerves on edge, my head spinning, my blood boiling, my . . .

No, that would never do.

Her revelation about her childhood explained a lot of things, especially her obsessive need to have her friends around all the time. But it didn't change the fact that he couldn't adjust to her manic activities and crowds, he couldn't fit into her slapdash life-style.

He turned the page of his paper, then turned it back after realizing he had no memory of what he'd read. Half his coffee had disappeared, too, with no memory of the taste. He shook his head. That was incomprehensible. How could he remember so well the taste of Emily's lips from two days ago and forget the flavor of something he'd drunk two minutes ago?

The door slammed below him. She never closed it quietly.

Leaning forward just a little, he watched over the top of his paper, waiting with equal amounts of trepidation and anticipation as her quick footsteps crossed the porch. But they stopped at the edge. She never entered his field of vision. She was probably sitting on the steps, wearing brightly colored shorts or ragged cutoffs, drinking a cola and eating something nauseating.

He wiped away the irrational smile that he discovered on his lips.

Maybe he should be polite, go down and say goodmorning. They had to speak sometime. They were going to be living under the same roof for at least a year.

Maybe that was how he should start the conversation.

Emily, we're going to be living under the same roof....

Before he could even get his newspaper folded, a little red car zipped into the driveway. Sam.

"I'm ready on time!" Emily shouted. She burst onto the yard, a flash of bright yellow and green, waving a tanned arm, her brown-gold hair bouncing.

"Did you know you've got a low tire over here?"

At the sound of Sam's voice, Carson tore his attention away from her and focused on him. He'd left his car and was standing on the far side of hers, looking down at the rear tire.

She went around and stood beside him. "It's okay. I'll take it to the service station tomorrow and fill it up. Let's go. We don't want to be late."

Sam crossed his arms over his chest. "I thought you were going to buy some new tires. The air's probably coming through the rubber, it's so thin."

"I am. I just haven't had time."

"Time? Or money?"

She folded her arms, too, and lifted her chin... proudly, he thought, and couldn't help but admire her independence.

He wanted to back away, to ignore the personal conversation taking place below him. But he remained transfixed, worried that Emily didn't have the money for new tires. Teachers didn't get paid a lot.

Though, of course, it was none of his concern.

"It's only been two weeks since you balanced my checkbook. You know how much I have."

Carson sucked in his breath. Good grief! Not only was she too irresponsible to balance her own checkbook, but she was willing to allow someone else to do something that private.

"I know how much you *had*," Sam drawled. "Two weeks is plenty of time for you to give away a lot more than what those tires cost."

She gave away her money? That's why she drove an old car and furnished her house with odds and ends, not because she was thrifty.

She shifted from one foot to the other. "I bought a new baseball bat for Jeremy. I still have the rest of it. I'll get the damned tires next week. I've been really busy, trying to get everything done for the end of school. Come on. They're waiting for us." She turned to go.

He grabbed her neck playfully in the crook of his arm. "I don't want to hear excuses. I want to see the gleam of new rubber."

"Nag, nag, nag." Laughing, she slipped out of his grasp and darted away, climbing into his car.

Carson watched them drive down the street. His accidental eavesdropping had resulted in more proof of Emily's total unsuitability. She had no place in his life.

Yet he resented Sam for his intrusion into Emily's privacy and envied him for having that right.

He took a sip of his coffee. It was stone cold, like the knot in the pit of his stomach.

How could she have kissed him so freely, seemed to give so much of herself, when she obviously had a close relationship with another man? So close, he had knowledge of her financial affairs.

He'd been right about Sam's proprietary air that first evening he'd met him. Yet he'd never seen any real evidence of an affair. And Emily wasn't the type to be sneaky. Or even circumspect. She was the most open, honest person he'd ever met.

Which wasn't always good, he reminded himself sternly. It was possible to be too open.

He went inside for another cup of coffee, then came back out and reopened his paper. With his tenant gone he could look forward to a day of uninterrupted peace and quiet. And that was good. He enjoyed peace and quiet and being alone.

He'd offered to take his grandmother shopping, but she had declined, saying she had other plans.

Emily's words suddenly came back to him. *They're waiting for us.*

He snapped the paper open. *They* probably meant his grandmother and Walter. At this point he supposed he could only hope for the best. Maybe the "discussion" he'd had with Emily last Sunday would discourage her continuing to involve his grandmother in dangerous activities. Surely, since Walter was his grandmother's age, they wouldn't be out playing football.

By early afternoon Carson was caught up on his company records and had tidied his apartment. He turned around in the middle of the living room and surveyed everything with satisfaction.

He sat down on the sofa, picked up a financial magazine and thumbed through it, then laid it back on the coffee table. He straightened the stack and moved them more completely into the center. He sat back, considered the arrangement, then decided to spread them out in an overlapping fashion.

He crossed his legs, draped his arm over the back of the sofa and drummed his fingers on the padded surface. The quiet in the room was a tangible, overpowering thing. He stood, crossed the room and turned on the stereo, sat back down and scowled to himself.

He loved quiet. What was going on here? Had he become so accustomed to Emily's incessant noise that his ears now expected it? That was a frightening thought. He could just see himself going to a city council meeting with a boom-box on his shoulder, snapping his fingers.

His own laughter startled him and appalled him.

Maybe he needed to get out for a while. Go...go where? Grandmother was out. His friends weren't the type he could call on the spur of the moment for a spontaneous outing.

So he'd go by himself. Take in a movie. Anything to get away from the sphere of Emily's influence, get his head back on straight.

But a rumble of thunder in the distance stopped him. Parting the curtains, he looked outside and saw that the sky had grown dark with the threat of rain. He hoped Emily and Celia didn't get caught in it. Maybe he'd better hang around, stick close to the phone, just in case.

He yanked the curtains closed.

That was a dumb idea. Even Emily had enough sense to come in out of the rain.

Nevertheless, he took down a book and settled in for the afternoon.

The Worlds of Fun tram stopped in their parking area, and the six of them dove into the warm rain. Sam and Walter ran ahead to open the doors of their respective cars.

"I think we're being ripped off," Jeremy shouted as he and Aaron veered toward Walter's car while Emily and Celia headed for Sam's.

"I know, but you got to do it before. Celia hasn't. Next time," Emily promised, then scrambled into the infinitesimal back seat. "The front seat's the best place," she assured Celia.

Sam climbed in, looked back at her and grinned. "Emily's easily amused," he said to Celia.

"You're the one who showed me," Emily countered.

"I'm easily amused, also," Celia said. "So do your stuff, Sam!"

He eased the car out of the parking lot, slowed by the masses of other people exiting because of the rain. When they finally reached the open highway, he revved the engine.

"Now! Do it now." Emily leaned forward, one hand on each of the front seats.

Celia, eyes sparkling, turned to give her a quick smile.

Sam hit a button, and the sunroof began rolling open. Emily pointed upward. Above their heads the rain came down but streamed across the roof almost horizontally.

"Cool, huh?" Emily shouted above the noise.

"Cool," Celia agreed.

"Stopping's a little tricky," Emily said, "but we're already soaked! A few more raindrops won't matter."

Sam leaned closer to the two of them to make himself heard. "It's only tricky if you wait until you stop before you close the sunroof. Emily's not one for planning ahead."

Emily shrugged unrepentantly, reached a hand through the open space into the rain to wave to Jeremy, Aaron and Walter in the car behind them, then settled back to enjoy the drive.

Conversation was difficult with the air and rain rushing overhead, and she was left alone with her thoughts. Too often of late she'd found Carson in those thoughts—and not just his hairy legs and chest. That was bad enough, but she could deal with that sort of thing. She might lust after Mel Gibson or Scott Bakula, but she never lost any sleep over them.

Carson, on the other hand, was rapidly turning into a real live person with a smile that, on those rare occasions it appeared, slid right from his lips into her heart. She'd had glimpses of his childhood, sat in the swing where he'd sat eating forbidden sweets, walked in the park where he'd played baseball and laughed. Against all logic, she wanted to find that child again.

She knew she was trying to make up for the fun of childhood she'd missed growing up, and that was okay. Fun was where you found it, and if Carson had found it once, he could find it again.

She scowled to herself and pulled her knees up under her chin, trying unsuccessfully to get comfortable in Sam's back seat. She knew only too well from past experience that you could lead a stodge to fun, but you couldn't make him enjoy it.

But that hadn't stopped her from wishing he'd been there to share the sensations when the Timberwolf roller coaster started its first stomach-floating dive downward or when they'd gone over the loop in the Orient Express and the sky had turned green with blue grass below...or when Celia had her first cotton candy in fifty years.

She'd insisted on the blue. "It only came in pink when I was young." Then they'd all teased her about her blue lips. So she'd had some pink to turn her lips a more acceptable purple.

Now Emily couldn't help imagining how he'd react to seeing the rain passing directly overhead. Though realistically she knew he'd probably be so busy worrying that the dampness would wrinkle his clothes, he'd miss the whole experience.

But maybe not, some stubborn imp whispered in her ear. Maybe Celia had been wrong when she'd written him off as a hopeless cause. She recalled the look of wonder in his eyes after he'd watched the lightning bug, and the way he'd sent the maple seed whirling after she'd showed him how. Maybe he only needed the right person to show him.

She thrust aside that potentially lethal thought and leaned forward between Celia and Sam. "When we get to your place, Sam, let's make a fire in the fireplace and roast wieners and marshmallows."

Sam lifted a thumb in agreement. "I have some great filets in the refrigerator if you can figure out how to keep them on a skewer."

Carson turned on the television, then turned it off, stood up, then sat down. He picked up the phone and dialed his grandmother's number again, listened to it ring ten times, then hung up.

The rain had poured, then it had stopped. The sun had come out again, then it had set. And still neither Emily nor his grandmother had come home. That pretty much confirmed his suspicion that they were together.

At least, he consoled himself, with the rain and now the darkness, they weren't likely to be playing football in the park.

He hoped.

At eleven o'clock, he went to bed, tossed and turned for a while, then finally drifted into an uneasy slumber. In his dreams Emily, wearing a neon yellow costume with matching feathered headgear, lured his grandmother, clad in neon purple, onto a high wire in the center ring of a circus. The two of them were doing fine, bowing and smiling to the applause, until Emily's headgear fell off and the feathers sheared the wire. Both women hung on, dangling above space, back and forth, lower and lower. Of course Emily didn't have a safety net. Suddenly she crashed to the ground with Celia tumbling after.

Carson sat bolt upright in bed, heart racing, pajamas glued to his skin with a cold sweat.

The crash. The downstairs door slamming. Yes, he was pretty sure he could hear noises from below. The faint sounds of rock music with a heavy beat pulsed up to him. Emily was home.

He checked the bedside clock. Nearly midnight. He'd like to call his grandmother and verify that she was home safely, too, but it was much too late for that. If anything was wrong, Emily would have let him know. *She'd* have no compunctions about disturbing someone in the middle of the night. He'd be rational tonight, then see Grandmother tomorrow for brunch.

He lay back down and was drifting into a relaxed slumber when another door slamming brought him upright again. The back door. Had she gone outside? In the middle of the night?

So what if she had?

He fluffed his pillow and dropped his head onto it. She could dance around naked in the moonlight for all he cared.

She was entirely capable of dancing around naked in the moonlight in his backyard.

He shot out of bed, opened the balcony doors as quietly as possible and tiptoed out.

Why was he sneaking around? he asked himself. Did he intend to stop her crazy actions or observe them?

She was fully clothed, walking around, looking at the ground, pausing occasionally. Once she seemed to be stepping off an area, measuring. Harmless. No reason for him to keep watching her. But he did.

In the moonlight she looked ethereal, like a fairy exploring her realm.

He shook his head, blinked rapidly. Where in the world had that thought come from? She wasn't a fairy. She was a schoolteacher with more than a few screws loose trying to make up for her lost childhood, walking around in the wet grass in the middle of the night in *his* backyard.

She paused beside the undamaged lilac bush. He cringed, fearing for the life of the plant.

She reached up, pulled down a branch and brought the blooms to her nose. As she tilted her face upward, he could see that her eyes were closed, her lips curved in a faint smile as she inhaled the fragrance.

He drew in a deep breath, smelling the same scent she smelled. His fingers tingled as though he could reach down and touch the silky skin of her face.

There was no other word for it. She looked ethereal, not of this world.

As though she could sense his gaze on her, her eyes opened and she looked directly into his. He took an involuntary step backward, away from the un- shielded vulnerability he saw there.

"Hi," she said, completely unperturbed at being caught wandering outside at midnight, sniffing the flowers.

"Hi," he answered, trying to match her nonchalance.

She loosed the branch and let it flip back up, dropping her hands to her sides. "They smell different at night, softer, more like moonlight than sunshine," she said as if that explained everything.

He started to point out that moonlight and sunshine had no odor, but he couldn't get the words out, couldn't disturb the naive belief on her face. Besides, hadn't he smelled sunshine on her towels? And looking down at her as she stood in the silvery blue darkness against the background of blossoms, he wasn't so sure moonlight was fragrance-free. For an incredible instant he seemed to catch a whiff of the silver moonlight that set her face aglow.

He moved back to the rail, cleared his throat and tried to clear his mind. "The grass is wet." The harshness of his words surprised him.

But not her. She lifted a glistening bare foot and smiled. "Not very. Come see."

For one crazy moment he actually considered doing it—going down to join her, walking across the damp grass in bare feet, holding the lilacs to his nose, touching her skin to see if the moonlight felt as silky as it looked.

Ridiculous. Of course he'd do no such thing. No matter how much he wanted to. What was wrong with him here lately that he seemed to be considering such irrational activities?

He answered his own question. It was her. Emily. She was contagious. Just like the measles.

"It's late," he said. "Good night."

"Good night." He thought—or wished—she sounded disappointed.

He turned away from her, went inside and closed the French doors behind him.

As he turned to lock them, he could see her through the panes of glass still standing there, only her face visible over the balcony rail from this distance. She was looking up, her head tilted to one side as if listening.

From somewhere in the deepest recesses of memory he recalled a story his grandmother had told him years ago. When the fairies had a wedding, the bluebells rang from midnight until dawn with the loveliest music ever heard.

He shook his head at his own foolishness and resisted the urge to open the doors and listen.

Emily took advantage of Carson's absence Sunday morning to hang the rest of her pictures. Her largest, the oil painting of springtime in the Ozarks, should go above the sofa, but she couldn't seem to get the hanger positioned right. Standing on the sofa, she was hammering it into its third location when hands grabbed her sides from behind and began to tickle her.

She shrieked, lost her balance and fell backward onto her attacker.

"Boy, you're a lot heavier than you look."

She struggled to her feet. "Jeremy! Are you all right? You scared me."

He bounced up, laughing, looking extremely pleased with himself. "Did you think I was a serial killer or something?"

"Or something. Serial killers don't normally tickle their victims to death. They smash their heads with a hammer!" She retrieved her weapon from the floor and waved it in the air.

"I'll remember that for next time. You sure were making a lot of noise in here. I knocked, but I guess you didn't hear me."

"Obviously not. As long as you're here, you can help me get this picture on the hanger."

"Jeez. First you try to mash me, then you put me to work."

While Emily held up the unwieldy painting, Jeremy slid the wire onto the hook.

"Now, I'll stand back, and you straighten it." She stepped off the sofa, across the room. "Left side up just a little. No, that's too much. There. Perfect."

Jeremy moved over beside her. "Man, you got your head on crooked if you think that picture's straight."

She ruffled his hair, draped an arm around his shoulders. "So bend your head over to the side when you look at it. Want something to drink?"

"Sure. You got any beer?"

"Sure. You got any ID?"

"Okay, okay. I'll settle for a cola."

"Hmm. Did I just get conned here?"

They went into the kitchen, and she took two soft drinks from the refrigerator. Through the open window, she saw a flash of silver go past.

"Oh, good. Carson and Celia are here." She handed Jeremy his soda. "Celia and I are going to get some flowers and plant them in the backyard. Want to help?"

"Yuck. It's muddy out there."

"You're washable. Come on. He probably let Celia out in front of the house."

As they entered the living room, she saw Celia crossing the porch. "Come on in," she called to her. "What did Carson say about planting flowers?" Surely he couldn't object to something as simple as that.

Celia rolled her eyes. "He said it's too muddy."

"I told you so," Jeremy said.

"Did you tell him it's already late in the season, and it's now or never?"

"I did. I think he just wants to be contrary. When he was little and didn't get his way, he'd stick that lip out and—"

"Grandmother!" Carson appeared on the other side of the screen door.

Celia glanced over her shoulder at him. "Someday your face is going to freeze in that scowl and you'll have to look at it every morning in the mirror when you shave. Trust me, it isn't an attractive expression. I'm going to slip into my old clothes, Emily, then I'll be ready to go. Would you excuse me?"

She headed for the bedroom with her large canvas bag.

Emily moved over to the door, gazing at Carson through the screen. He was clearly upset, not at all the same man who'd looked at her so tenderly the night before, the man whose expression had been so wistful she'd dared to ask him to join her.

"Will you come help us pick out plants?" she invited impulsively. "After all, you have to look at them, too."

He lowered his head and raked a hand through his hair. "Do you know what a mess this is going to be?"

"You're washable," Jeremy declared, and Emily couldn't suppress a giggle.

He lifted his hands in resignation. "Okay. I'll go get my car. I'll help you pick them out, but I'm not going to plant them."

Chapter Eight

At the nursery Carson followed the two of them in, but Emily didn't expect him to participate in the selection. She'd only asked him so he wouldn't feel left out, hadn't really believed he'd come along.

"Let's get some petunias," she suggested, pausing beside the table of colorful plants.

"Oh, yes. I've always loved petunias," Celia agreed. "The pink ones are nice."

"And the deep purple."

"The slugs love petunias, too," Carson interposed. "With this wet weather, that could be a problem. You'll have to put out a saucer of beer."

Emily smiled, started to laugh at what she assumed was a joke, but Celia's voice stopped her. "Yes, you're probably right. But I'm sure we can come up with a bit of beer for the creatures. Get some of the white petunias, too, Emily. They'll make a striking contrast."

"Beer?"

"Mmm-hmm." Celia handed Carson an empty flat and began loading plants onto it. "I usually have some zinnias and marigolds. What do you think?"

"Absolutely. And geraniums. Aren't the peach ones pretty?"

As they filled the flats, Carson carried them to the checkout counter and gamely returned for more. After the third trip when he returned to where they were sorting through the geraniums, he finally protested.

"Don't you think that's enough?"

"Soon, dear," Celia murmured.

Emily looked up and gave him a reassuring smile, resisting an urge to pat him on the head. He looked so serious, so concerned, standing like an immaculate statue amid all the tables overflowing with lush greenery and brilliant flowers. "It's all right. I measured last night. We have plenty of space."

He shook his head unbelievingly and sighed. "What the heck. You'd better get some begonias for that shady corner."

Emily's smile widened at this active participation.

"He's right," Celia admitted. "And a few ferns, don't you think, dear? You always loved ferns."

Finally they were ready to check out. As they waited in line, a table of plants on the vegetable side caught Emily's eye. "One more," she begged.

"No!" Carson groaned. "Trust me. You don't have the room."

But she'd already darted over and picked up two pots. Turning back, she held up one in each hand. "This will be so cool. Just think, we'll be able to go out in the backyard and pick our very own tomatoes."

"That's a lovely idea," Celia agreed.

Carson jammed his hands into his pockets and looked straight ahead. Emily exchanged a glance with Celia, and both smothered a giggle.

But, she had to concede, Carson was being remarkably agreeable—even helpful with his practical advice about the slugs and beer and about the begonias in shady spots.

When they arrived home, he didn't even complain that one of the pots had tipped over, spilling soil in the previously immaculate trunk of his car. He helped to carry the plants into the yard, then looked dubiously at first the multitude of pots, then the flower beds.

· Emily's gaze followed his, and she stood on one foot, then the other. The beds did look smaller than she remembered.

"Jeremy, come help me get the tools from the basement," Carson said, his tone resigned.

Jeremy trotted after him, and the pair soon returned with a wide assortment of tools. Without another word, Carson began turning over the soil with a gardening fork. "Well, you're lucky," he said, examining it, "the rain was hard and fast. A lot of it ran off. Still..." He shook his head.

Jeremy walked over, plunged a hand into the loosened earth. "Oh, yuck. This feels like—"

"Don't say it," Emily warned.

"You don't know what I was going to say." He grinned.

"And I don't want to know. Just grab some plants and get to work."

Jeremy picked up a pot of begonias and tugged on the greenery.

"No, no," Carson said. "You're going to break the plant. Here, let me show you." In his relatively immaculate clothes, he sank to the grass beside Jeremy.

A couple of hours later the beds were packed full and several of the plants remained in pots.

"Your system of measurement contains a few inaccuracies," Carson said, sitting down beside Emily and wiping some of the mud from his hands onto the grass.

"I admit, it hasn't received government approval."

This was the most relaxed she'd ever seen him. After a brief period of trying to stay clean, he'd given up, joined in, and now seemed quite comfortable with mud splattered all over his gray shorts and shirt, trapped in the hair of his bare legs, and mixed with blades of grass on his hands.

And it was the most appealing she'd ever seen him.

"We'll make some hanging baskets with the leftovers," Celia promised. She stood and rinsed off the majority of the mud with the garden hose.

"Do me." Jeremy offered his caked hands and feet, and she turned the stream of water on him.

"I'm going to go in, wash up and change clothes," Celia said when Jeremy was relatively clean.

"I'm thirsty. Can I have another soda?" Jeremy asked.

"Oh, I suppose so. I guess you've earned it."

Carson picked up the hose as Celia and Jeremy disappeared into the house.

"A tape measure might improve your accuracy next time," Carson suggested.

And she couldn't resist. Before he could get to his feet, she lifted her muddy hands to his face and slid them down his cheeks, then touched his nose, depositing a dollop.

He stared at her in amazement, and for a moment she thought he was going to be angry. Well, it had been worth it.

But he blinked twice, dropped the water and splatted his hands in the nearest flower bed to get fresh mud. He turned to her, a wicked gleam in his eyes, and put a hand on each side of her face, holding her longer than was really necessary. For a moment she thought he was going to kiss her again. Her lips tingled at the thought.

But he looked away and duplicated her actions instead, smudging mud on her nose. When he dropped his hands to the grass again, she leaned over for more muck. He moved with her, scooping it out of her hands as fast as she could grab it.

"This is war!" she said, giggling.

"Is that right?" He laughed and grabbed her arms, stroking up and down, smearing her thoroughly.

"Oo-oo, you're going to be *so* sorry!" She flung herself at him, pushing him backward onto the wet, slippery grass, landing on his chest, clutching his shoulders.

He flopped over, taking her with him, and they were lying side by side. As they grappled, somehow his arms were around her, his muddy face only inches from hers. They were still smiling, but no longer laughing.

With one finger he traced along her ribs, down the edge of her breast. His eyes, their color echoing the grass and trees around them, never left hers.

Her body tingled where he touched her, strained toward him, wanting the touching to go on, wanting him to touch her with his whole hand, his body.

From far away the phone was ringing but, oddly enough, she couldn't think of anyone she wanted to talk to at the moment.

Her lips parted, anticipating—

"Emily, telephone," Celia called.

The door slammed, and Emily sat bolt upright. From the corner of her eye, she saw Carson do the same.

Jeremy charged out and grabbed the forgotten hose, bringing it over to her. "You're all dirty. I'll wash you off."

"Okay," she agreed, still a little dizzy and breathless. The first stream of water hit her in the face, bringing her at least partially back to reality. "Only my hands and feet!" she shrieked.

When she was sufficiently clean not to ruin the floors, she ran into the house and grabbed the phone. "Hello?"

"Emily James?"

"Yes."

"Is Jeremy over there? This is his mother." She sounded angry.

"Yes, Mrs. Miller, he's here."

"Do you think you could send him home? I've been trying to find him all day."

"I'm sorry. I assumed he'd told you he was coming here. I'll bring him right now."

"I would appreciate that."

She hung up and stared at the instrument. The woman probably hadn't been there when Jeremy had left that morning. How could he have told her where he was going? Anger flared inside her. How could a mother do that to her son?

She tried to tamp down the irritation. There was nothing she could do but be Jeremy's friend—and get him back as quickly as possible.

She went outside again. To her amazement, Jeremy and Carson were having a good-natured battle with the hose. Both were soaking wet.

"That was your mom, kiddo," she told him. "I need to get you home."

He shrugged and surrendered the water to Carson. "Yeah, okay." He didn't seem overly enthused about the prospect.

"Me, too," Celia said, coming outside dressed in the pantsuit she'd worn to brunch. "Will someone please take me home? I'm exhausted."

"Don't you want to stay for dinner?" Emily asked.

"Not this time." She did look unusually tired. "I still haven't recovered from yesterday."

Carson's brow furrowed in concern as he looked at his grandmother. "Are you all right?"

"I'm fine. Just tired."

"What did you do yesterday that was so tiring?" he asked suspiciously.

Celia, Emily and Jeremy exchanged glances, and Jeremy giggled.

Celia straightened her shoulders, looking regal. "We went to Worlds of Fun."

"What?"

"We went to Worlds of Fun. Do you have a hearing problem? You're awfully young for that."

He stepped over to her, took her arm. "What did you do at Worlds of Fun?" He directed a glare toward Emily.

"Oh, stop it. The trip was my idea. Ever since they built the place, I've wanted to go. And I thoroughly enjoyed myself. I plan to go back."

For a moment the two stared at each other, and Emily wasn't sure who'd win. But Carson abdicated, dropped Celia's arm and turned away.

"Let's go upstairs and I'll change into some dry clothes, then take you home."

As he drove back from taking Celia home, Carson found himself alone with his disturbing thoughts. He'd acted like a child, rolling around in the mud with Emily. Well, not exactly a child, he amended as he remembered how her body had felt against his, how the adrenaline had surged from the activity and from her nearness, blending together until he couldn't tell where one cause stopped and the other began.

But, he admitted to himself, it had been enjoyable. For a few crazy minutes he'd forgotten himself, his clothes, his position in life, and indulged in undignified, childish behavior.

Good grief! He'd been right. Emily was contagious, and he'd better watch himself or the next thing he knew, he'd be acting as scatterbrained as she.

When he returned home, he found Emily sitting on the front steps, elbows on her knees, chin on her hands. She sat up straight, alert. She'd obviously been waiting for him.

"Is Celia okay?" she asked.

He hesitated in midstep, one foot on the step where she sat. He could hear the concern in her voice, see it in her eyes. With a sigh he gave up thoughts of a hasty escape and sank down beside her but stared straight ahead, toward Mrs. Johnson's house, avoiding Emily's unguarded expression.

"I think so," he assured her. "Grandmother's not young. She tires more easily than you."

"I was worried she'd make herself sick. She ate an awful lot of junk food yesterday. Had to try everything at least once. Twice if she liked it. And then steak and marshmallows—lots of marshmallows—at Sam's house."

So they'd gone to Sam's house when they had gotten rained out. And eaten . . . "Steak and marshmallows?" He turned to look at her.

She smiled. "Not together. Although I suppose they get together in your stomach afterward. Anyway, if I'd eaten everything she did, it would have made me sick."

"This is serious. I wasn't aware we had enough junk food in America to make you sick. I should think by now you'd be immune to the most massive dose."

Her eyes widened in surprise, then she burst into delighted laughter. "You're teasing me."

"I suppose I am." She didn't have to sound so shocked. He wasn't *that* stodgy.

"I was afraid you'd be upset with me for taking Celia to the amusement park."

"I am well aware of how stubborn Grandmother can be. If she says it was her idea, I guess I can't really blame you." He looked away from her again, leaned down and picked up a small stick. "Though you could have tried to talk her out of it, or told me so I could try, or at least not let her eat everything in sight." He snapped the stick in half, trying to quell the frustration he felt building—frustration with her, his grandmother, himself.

"Your grandmother is an adult with a mind of her own, not some child to be told what to do."

He tossed the broken stick into the yard and turned to face her again. Her eyes were wide, totally without guile. It was hard to be irritated with her, though sometimes it was impossible not to be.

"Older people do become childlike, Emily. You can't tell me you don't know that."

Her chin lifted slightly in that obstinate way she had. "Certainly I know that. But not your grandmother. Her mind's as sharp as yours. Maybe she doesn't hear every whisper, but we should always speak in a clear, distinct voice anyway."

"She forgets things."

Emily arched an eyebrow. "And you never do?"

He threw his hands up. "Of course I do. It's not the same thing."

"Your grandmother doesn't any more need to be in a retirement home than I do," she snapped.

That remark touched a nerve. He'd battled with himself a long time before recommending the move to his grandmother. "It was a mutual decision. We both feel more comfortable when she has someone around all the time, help available when she needs it. I used to worry when I was at work that something would happen to her, that she'd fall and break a hip or have a heart attack and die before I got home."

She laid a warm hand on his arm, suddenly contrite. "I know you love her and want the best for her. It's just..." Her gaze slid away from his face, over his shoulder, became unfocused.

"Just what?" he asked, though he wasn't sure he wanted to know.

She blinked, came back to him. "She's so vital and alive and so interested in everything. She's just not ready for a retirement home. And if you're trying to psychoanalyze me, yes, I'm sure part of my friendship with your grandmother is because I don't have one. I was part of a family long enough to know how it felt, and I miss it, so I've created my own. But all the members of my created family are nonspecific. They're friends. And Celia would still be my friend if she were twenty-four instead of eighty-four.''

He didn't doubt that for a minute. Her friends ran the gamut. "Wasn't there anyone who stayed in your life long enough to qualify as a parent?" An eccentric Auntie Mame-type, no doubt.

She shrugged. "I stayed with Sam's parents the longest. In fact, I guess I lied. Sam's the exception to the rule. He has a specific slot. He's my brother."

Carson leaned back against the porch column. The late-afternoon sun seemed to have brightened to midday brilliance at that news. "Your brother?"

"He fancies he's my big brother. Sometimes he gets on my nerves trying to take care of me. But..." She sighed exaggeratedly and rolled her eyes. "Like you with your grandmother, he means well."

He was going to have to give some thought, some analytical thought, to the thrill he experienced upon receiving that information.

"Your brother," he said again.

"Yeah. Can't you see the family resemblance?" She grinned impudently. "We both have two hands, two feet, two eyes, one nose."

And that, he thought, pretty much summed up the criteria for admission to Emily's family. Which made him eligible. Except he didn't want to be a nonspecific member. He had quite definite ideas of the role he desired, and it wasn't that of brother.

"How many different families did you live with?" he asked, forcing his thoughts away from the errant direction they'd taken.

"Six." She grinned wryly—a little sadly, he thought, though it was hard to think of Emily as sad. "I was a difficult child. I wanted my real parents back, not a substitute. I was almost sixteen when I went to live with Sam's family, and I'd settled down a lot by that time. Plus, they're wonderful people."

"Wonderful people, but still not a substitute for your own family," he speculated.

"Of course not. By then I'd accepted that my family was gone and there'd never be an adequate substitute. I love Sam's parents for who they are."

"Just like your thousand other friends."

Her grin turned impish. "At last count, there were only about nine hundred."

And not an adequate substitute among them, he thought, understanding her compulsive need for friends a little better.

"Want to come in and have some dinner?" she invited, and he sensed she was inviting him to join her self-made family. "I'll cook since you were so nice about helping us put in the flowers."

A brief vision flitted through his head of a candlelight dinner with a crisp salad, delicately seasoned entrée and buttered vegetables, then making love with the glow of candles on tanned skin. But it vanished immediately to be replaced by one of cold pizza with sardines and making love on that water bed with all the lights on. Actually, he could probably handle the first part if he knew the last part was waiting.

He stood abruptly. What was he thinking about? She'd just confessed to him that she was alone in the world, had a need for love, was every bit as vulnerable as she looked. He could make love to her all night, but what would they do when morning came? He couldn't offer her anything beyond that. He might understand her eccentric behavior, but that didn't mean he could ever be a part of it. He was no longer a child free to have fun visiting his grandmother. He was a responsible adult—all the time. She'd make him crazy before noon.

Well, his libido argued, *you could leave before dawn*.

But he couldn't. The best thing he could do would be to leave *before dinner*.

"Thanks," he said, "but I have plans." Which meant he'd have to get dressed and leave the house so she wouldn't know he was lying.

The disappointment that crossed her face told him he was doing the right thing. Better a little now than a lot later. Never mind the disappointment that sagged through his gut.

"Well, have a good one." Emily went inside and headed straight for the telephone. But for a moment, as she listened to Carson's footsteps going up the stairs, she couldn't remember a single phone number.

His plans probably included that redhead. Not that she cared. She had plenty of friends. She wouldn't be alone this evening, either. She didn't need him.

But Olga was out to dinner. Jeannie had a date. Rose was preparing a proposal for a business meeting on Monday. Teri was out dancing. Darlene had gone bowling, Jon's line was busy, and so was Collins's. She already knew Celia was tired....

Finally she gave up. She could spend an evening by herself. She'd done it before. Last winter when she'd had the flu, she hadn't wanted anyone around.

This evening she'd treat herself. She'd order a pizza with double anchovies, catch up on her reading, take a bubble bath, enjoy her own company.

She flipped on the television and phoned in the pizza order, then slumped onto the sofa. Shuffling through the paper, she found the classifieds and scanned the pet section.

Oh, my. She'd never realized there were so many little animals that needed a home.

But Carson had said she could have a cat, singular. He hadn't even addressed the subject of dogs or ferrets or cockatoos.

She threw the paper aside. If she had only one animal, it would be alone all day while she worked. That wouldn't be fair. Next time she saw Carson, she'd ask if it was all right to get more than one so they could keep each other company. Surely if one was acceptable, he wouldn't object to two. Or three.

After she finished her pizza, Emily went out in the backyard to admire their handiwork. She'd never had flower beds before, or her very own tomato source.

The plants were all still alive—thriving, she thought. Most of them already had a few blossoms. Soon they'd be a riot of color. She'd get some pots tomorrow and plant the leftovers. They deserved a chance to live, too.

She pulled her chair over close to the burned lilac bush—the one nearest the fence—so she could enjoy the fragrance, and opened her book.

The evening was turning dusky when Carson came home—alone, she noticed from her vantage point in the backyard. He couldn't have had a very wild evening with that redhead, or he wouldn't be back so early. The thought buoyed her spirits.

She hurried inside to turn off her stereo. She'd cranked it up pretty loud to be able to hear it in the backyard, and Carson probably wouldn't appreciate that. Patting herself on the back for being so considerate, such a good tenant, she went back outside. Maybe he'd come out on the balcony as he'd done before and she could ask him about the pets. Maybe this time he'd even come down and join her.

A delicious shiver darted through her as she remembered the look in his eyes as he'd smeared her body with mud, the feel of his hands on her arms, his finger tracing her ribs, the side of her breast.

A light came on in the kitchen, but she couldn't tell what he was doing. The blinds in the kitchen window and on the French doors of the balcony were tightly closed.

She picked up a tiny pebble and aimed it at the French doors.

No response.

She tossed another, a little larger. And another. To her dismay, the fourth pebble, no longer quite so tiny, crashed through the glass.

She could probably forget about the two cats.

Chapter Nine

The outside light came on, the door burst open, and Carson charged onto the balcony, his face darker than the rapidly falling shadows. Not exactly the scene she'd had in mind.

"Hi," she said quietly, lifting a hand in a weak wave. "I'll pay for the window."

"Emily?" He leaned over the rail and peered down.

"I'm afraid so. I'm sorry about the accident."

"You're the one who threw a rock through my window?"

She nodded, wishing she could shrink to a size small enough to hide in the grass. "Yes. I did it."

"Are you lying to protect someone? Is Jeremy down there with you?"

"No. It was me."

He ducked his head and ran a hand through his hair, a gesture that was becoming distressingly familiar. "Why did you throw a rock through my window?"

"To get your attention."

"You certainly got it."

"Well, have a good evening." She sidled toward the house. "Let me know about the cost on that glass."

"Emily! Come back here." He leaned farther over the balcony rail. "Surely you didn't throw a rock through my window simply to wish me a good evening."

"We'll talk about it later. My phone's ringing."

Just before she closed the door behind her, she could hear him saying something, but she had no desire to find out what.

She answered her phone, but for once her heart wasn't in the conversation and she ended it as soon as politely possible. Flopping onto the sofa, she turned on the television, more for background noise than from any interest in the program.

From the day she'd moved in, her presence had spelled disaster for Carson. If, as Celia had said, there'd been no hope for his learning to enjoy life before she met him, there was even less now. She'd undoubtedly made the situation worse instead of better.

And reminding herself that she shouldn't become involved with him was completely unnecessary. That wasn't even an option. There was no way he'd ever become involved with a perpetual accident. So she didn't need to worry that he'd want to exclude her friends from her life. He'd be much more likely to accept her friends and exclude her!

All things considered, she ought to be glad she'd broken his window so he hadn't come down to touch her and hold her and kiss her again. She was already having enough trouble trying to convince herself his touches and his kiss weren't as wonderful as she remembered, didn't really fill her mind to the exclusion of everything else.

She turned off the television and went to bed. If she dreamed about him, what the heck. She had to dream about something. Why shouldn't he disrupt her sleeping hours as well as her waking?

When Carson pulled into his driveway Monday evening he noticed that Emily's car still had a low tire. He shook his head as he drove past. This irresponsible person was teaching the leaders of tomorrow.

Though he had to admit she did have a kind of charm that probably made all the kids love her and hang on every word.

He put his car in the garage and slammed the door closed. All the more reason she ought to learn a little responsibility.

Clutching his heavy briefcase, he trudged across the porch and upstairs. She didn't rush out and tackle him or throw rocks at him, so he supposed he ought to be grateful. Martin would be arriving soon to pick up some important papers, and he could only hope she'd extend the same courtesy to him.

Tossing his briefcase onto the sofa, he walked straight through his living room and onto the balcony as if drawn by a magnetic force . She was sitting in the yard, her back to him, head bent over some task, singing softly to herself.

Cautiously, quietly, he moved closer to the rail, peering over. She was potting the rest of the flowers. Well, that was good. He hated to see anything go to waste.

He watched for an extra moment, taking pleasure in her movements as she worked with the flowers. She handled them as she did her friends—lovingly. She really wasn't a bad person, he thought. Just a little flaky.

A lot flaky, he reminded himself, forcing himself to look away from her and go back inside. He still had a little work to get done on the documents before Martin arrived. He opened the briefcase and settled down to business. Knowing Emily was occupied with something conventional gave him a safe, contented feeling.

Or maybe, a small voice whispered in the back of his head, *it's just knowing she's there—a happy, sexy presence in your backyard, only a few feet away.* But he dismissed that ridiculous small voice and concentrated on his work.

When Martin arrived an hour later, he had everything ready.

"Got time for a drink?" Carson asked, handing him the documents, hoping for no good reason that he'd refuse.

"Sure. I can always make time for a drink. Scotch on the rocks?"

"You got it."

Martin sat down on the sofa and leafed through the documents. "I see you haven't been able to get rid of your wild and crazy schoolteacher."

The bottle Carson was pouring from rattled against the glass at Martin's words. "What do you mean?" What had she done now?

Martin laughed in a smug, leering way Carson didn't think he liked. "The cops were pounding on her door when I came in. I thought you'd probably called them."

Carson's hand shook as he handed Martin his drink. "The police? No, I didn't call them."

"You know, it really doesn't look good to have somebody like that living so close. You have a public image to think about."

Carson sank into his recliner and tossed down half his own drink. Martin's words came to his ears as if through a long tunnel. What were the police doing at Emily's door? What had happened now? Who could have called them? When he found out, he'd certainly have a talk with that person. Maybe Emily did a few off-the-wall, irritating things, but nothing really bad or illegal. Why would anyone call the cops?

"Let's hope they're not down there for a drug search," Martin said.

What was the man talking about? "Drugs? Emily would never do drugs."

Martin shrugged and sipped his drink. "Everybody does drugs. It's just a question of whether you're smart enough not to get caught. But I can guarantee it'll make the headlines if the tenant of a city councilman, someone who lives in the same building with him, gets busted. You know how the media loves dirt."

Carson stood and paced across the room, looked out the front window at the squad car parked in the street in front of his house. "She doesn't do drugs," he said firmly. He was as positive of that as he was of his own habits. She'd never do anything that would be such a bad example for the kids.

Besides, she was spacey enough already. She didn't need drugs. She was high on life.

"The police can come to your house for other reasons besides arresting you," Carson said, speaking as much to himself as to Martin.

"I guess that's possible. Somebody in her family could have been murdered. Still not good publicity."

"Or killed in a car wreck. Her parents—no, they're dead." One of her friends, Sam, Jeremy. . .

Emily could be downstairs right this minute listening to the words of some police officer, a stranger, as he told her someone she loved was lying in a hospital, bleeding, or already dead. Or that officer could be putting handcuffs on her slim, tanned wrists, dragging her to a jail cell for something she hadn't meant to do.

"Well, it's too late to do anything about it now," Martin said. "All you can do is hope it's nothing major, then get her out of there as fast as possible."

Carson whirled around to stare at the man sitting there so calmly, passing judgment on someone he knew nothing about. He had to get rid of him, had to get to Emily. Whatever had happened, she needed a friend. She always needed a friend. She couldn't face this crisis alone.

"Well, you be sure and let me know if you have any questions about those documents," Carson said. "Good to see you again. Let's get together for lunch soon."

Martin paused with his drink suspended in midair halfway to his mouth, a startled look on his face.

That couldn't be helped. Emily was in some sort of trouble, and he needed to get down there. He opened the door and stood impatiently beside it. "I'll owe you one. Or take the bottle."

"Are you all right?" Martin asked.

"Of course." What was the matter with the man? Why was he lingering when it was obviously time to go?

Martin rose, setting his glass on the coffee table, his brow furrowed in concern. "You're sure?"

Carson frowned. "Certainly I'm sure. What makes you think otherwise?"

"Nothing. No reason." Martin moved toward the door, in slow motion, it seemed.

Finally he was out the door. Carson walked down the stairs with him, marveling that he'd never before noticed Martin's tendency to creep along like he was a hundred years old. On the porch he pumped his associate's hand rapidly and released it. "Give me a call if you have any questions. So long."

And he was at last free to check on Emily.

As he approached her door, two police officers came out.

"Appreciate your help, ma'am," one said, and they walked away, gun belts creaking.

At least they weren't taking her away. But the look of distress on her face as she stood in the doorway holding the screen open told him something was wrong.

"Carson, what's the matter?" she asked when his eyes met hers.

That wasn't right. She'd taken his question.

"Nothing. What did they want?" He jerked his thumb over his shoulder in the direction of the squad car.

"Come on in," she invited, standing aside.

He stepped into her living room and turned to face her. His arms of their own volition extended out to her.

Without hesitation she fell into them, laying her head on his chest. "Jeremy's run away from home," she said, her voice shaky, muffled against the folds of his white cotton shirt.

He slowly let out his breath; didn't want to let her know how relieved he felt. The news was bad, and he knew she was upset, but she wasn't going to jail, no one was dead or even seriously wounded. Happiness swelled inside him. Of course, some of that happiness could be because she felt so good in his arms. Too good. His feelings were inappropriate for the situation.

"He didn't come to school today," she continued. "I called his mother when she got home to see if he was sick, but she didn't know where he was. He'd left for school just like always. What if something's happened to him? You hear such horror stories."

He stroked her soft hair. "He'll be fine. He's probably at the movies with a friend."

She shook her head. "Not for the whole day." Suddenly she backed away. "Oh, dear. I'm wrinkling your shirt and tie. I'm sorry."

He wanted to pull her back, tell her it didn't matter, to wrinkle away—whatever it took to give her back her smile. But he forced himself to do the smart thing, to let her go.

She flopped onto the sofa. "The police are checking everybody, but I'm the one he'd come to if he had a problem. I even gave him a key in case he needed to get in when I was gone. He'd come here. If he could." She mumbled the last ominously.

He sat down beside her. "Don't jump to conclusions until you know something for sure. I have some really smooth brandy upstairs. Why don't I go get it, and you can have a drink and try to relax?"

She shook her head. "I need to keep my mind clear in case... well, just in case."

He felt completely helpless—an unusual and unpleasant sensation. "Then how about some pizza and cola?" It was the only thing he could think of that might interest her.

"Yes, I think I could use a soda."

She started to get up, but he laid a hand on her arm. "I'll get it for you. I know where the refrigerator is." He tried a smile and was vastly relieved when she returned it.

Emily leaned back on the sofa, amazed at how much better she felt just having Carson there. When he'd held her, the pain and fear had seemed to diminish by half. But that was always the case when a friend shared the problem, she reminded herself. It didn't mean Carson mattered more than her other friends.

But it had felt extra-special good when he'd wrapped her in his arms.

Carson stuck his head back in the living room. "You're out of soft drinks. I'll just run to the convenience store and pick up a six-pack."

She frowned. "That's odd. I could have sworn I had plenty. Did you check the vegetable bin?"

"No. How could I have overlooked something so obvious?"

She followed him back into the kitchen.

But the vegetable bin yielded only a couple of beers.

"This is crazy. I always keep lots of sodas cold in case company drops in."

"Well, apparently you didn't this time."

"Yes, I did. This morning when I grabbed a can on the way to work, there was a whole bunch left. You don't suppose somebody broke in and stole—"

"Jeremy!" they both exclaimed at the same time.

"You said he has a key," Carson reminded her.

"And he loves sodas. But that still doesn't tell us where he is now."

"Shh-hh." He lifted one finger. "Listen."

"To what? I don't hear anything."

"It sounds like a television. I heard it before and thought it was coming from your bedroom."

"I don't have a television in my bedroom. I thought it was coming from your place."

He shook his head. "Come on. I think I may know where we can find some answers."

She followed him outside, down the steps and over to the basement door.

"The lock's been jimmied," he said, indicating new scratches on the wood facing. "When he went with me yesterday to get the tools, he would have seen all the old furniture we have stored down there, including a black-and-white television."

"If he's in there, I'm going to kill him."

Carson flung the door wide, and the sounds became louder. Halfway across the room, against one wall, light flickered into the dimness. Emily thought she saw movement in a large old chair that was losing its stuffing.

"Jeremy?"

Carson went down the steps, reached overhead and pulled a string, switching on a bare light bulb, illuminating the room.

A small blond head crouched down in the chair. Angry and relieved, Emily raced across the room to him and knelt on the concrete floor in front of him. He turned away from her, refused to look at her. A thousand thoughts raced through her head, and she had to remind herself to stay calm.

"It's all right. Just tell me what happened. Why did you run away? Why are you hiding from me? Your mother's worried sick about you."

He snorted at the last remark, but finally spoke. "No, she's not. As long as she has that goon around, she doesn't need me."

"Of course she does. Are you telling me you ran away because you're jealous of your mother's boyfriend?"

"He was there when I got home last night," he mumbled. "We had a fight. She always takes his side."

A chill ran down Emily's spine. "A fight? Jeremy, did he hit you?"

He didn't answer. Gently but firmly she turned his face toward her. Behind her she heard Carson gasp. She bit her lip to keep from expressing her horror at the bruise on the side of his head, the swollen black eye. "Let's go upstairs and put some ice on that," she said softly.

"It's okay," he protested, but allowed her to lead him out of the basement and into her living room.

She went into the kitchen to put some ice cubes in a plastic bag. Carson was just coming in the door after closing up the basement.

"I guess I'll go on home and leave you two alone," he said.

"Please don't." The words left her mouth before she realized she was going to say them. She didn't want him to take away the support and warmth she felt from him. She desperately needed him with her.

He took her free hand. "All right. I won't."

Emily closed the door and leaned weakly against it, looking at Carson. "I think I'll take you up on that brandy if you're still offering."

He grinned. "I'll bring back the bottle. I could use a drop or two myself."

For a few seconds she stood unmoving, drained of emotional energy, basking in the intimacy of his gaze, his closeness. Abruptly she stood upright, feeling foolish. "Oh, I guess I have to stop blocking the door before you can get out."

"I'll be right back." He placed one finger under her chin, bent forward and touched her lips lightly with his.

"Okay," she whispered, stepping aside, allowing him to leave.

Feeling even weaker than before, she made her way to the sofa and sank down. This had certainly been an eventful evening—and it would appear the main event was only warming up.

Carson had been totally supportive with Jeremy, especially when his mother arrived in complete hysterics. She had been horrified at her son's injuries, at first blaming Emily, refusing to accept the possibility that her boyfriend had done it. For a while there, she'd thought Carson was going to bodily throw the woman out. The memory brought a smile to her face. Having somebody stand up for her was a pleasurable experience.

When Mrs. Miller had assured Jeremy that she did love him and would certainly never see Fred again, he agreed to go home with her. Emily had gone outside with them and detained her until Jeremy got in the car.

"You know I have a responsibility to report this to the authorities," Emily had told the woman. "They'll investigate and, unless you get rid of Fred, you could lose Jeremy. And I promise you that if anything like this ever happens again, I'll do everything in my power to take him away from you."

Tears had welled in Mrs. Miller's eyes. "It won't happen again," she'd whispered. "Fred won't be back. I promise you that. I guess I've had my priorities a little screwed up."

Emily leaned back on the sofa and propped her feet on the coffee table. She ought to get up, comb her hair, put on a little lipstick, make herself presentable, but she really didn't have the energy. Besides, even as disheveled as she was, she wasn't covered in mud, and that hadn't seemed to bother Carson yesterday.

A light tap sounded on the door.

"Come in," she called, still not moving.

He entered with a bottle of brandy and two snifters ... minus his tie and suit jacket. He even had the top button of his shirt undone, allowing a few hairs to peek out. She couldn't restrain a giggle as he sat down beside her, opened the bottle and poured two drinks.

He turned his attention to her at the sound, raising a questioning eyebrow.

"You still don't look casual," she said. "I'll bet you even look dignified when you're naked in the shower." She started to laugh, but the laughter died in midstream as she realized what she'd said, as a picture of Carson standing naked, wet and aroused filled her mind.

He grinned suggestively as he handed her one of the drinks and set the other on the coffee table. Leaning over, he pulled off his shoes and socks, then propped his feet on the table beside hers. "How's this? Am I approaching casual yet?"

"Well," she said nervously, "that's closer, I suppose."

He picked up his glass and touched it to hers. "Here's to casualness."

She sipped the amber liquid, letting the warmth slide down her throat. "This is good."

"Do you think Jeremy's going to be all right?" he asked, swirling his brandy.

"I think so. His mother just got a pretty big shock. She seems ready to make some long-needed changes."

He nodded. He seemed to be closer to her, though she hadn't noticed him moving. Maybe she was just becoming more and more aware of his nearness after visualizing him nude.

"You handled that situation incredibly well," he said.

"Huh? What situation?" Was he reading her mind, her lascivious thoughts?

"Jeremy's venture into the world."

"Oh. Thank you." She needed to mark this day on her calendar. She'd done something right when Carson was around.

"I was worried about you when I saw the police down here."

She laughed softly. "When I first opened the door and saw the officer, I thought you'd called the police because I broke your window."

He grinned and shook his head. "You amaze me. Most of the time you come off like a total flake, surrounded by more flakes, including my grandmother. You eat pizza for breakfast and hang pictures at midnight. Then today happens and you're suddenly a mature, in-charge person. I don't quite know what to make of you, Emily James."

Emily wasn't sure if it was the liquor, Carson's words, or his proximity, but she was becoming very warm and relaxed. "I'm not so hard to figure out. I just like to enjoy life."

"The way you didn't have a chance to do when you were growing up."

She shifted uncomfortably and took another sip of her brandy. "It's possible to have a good time on both ends of your life, you know. You might want to try it sometime."

"I just might," he said softly, his gaze slowly stroking her from head to foot, heating every place it touched.

"I didn't mean—" she began, then stopped as he dropped his feet to the floor, took the glass from her and set it on the table beside his. Slowly, deliberately, he slid his arms around her and pulled her to him, his lips descending to hers, escalating the heat to a raging fire.

Her breath caught in her throat, and she sent up a silent prayer of thanks that she hadn't finished her sentence. Maybe she did mean that after all.

He leaned closer, and for a moment seemed to lose his balance, shifting against her. But he caught himself on the end table, steadied and lifted one hand to cup her cheek, nibbling gently on her lower lip, stroking her lips with his tongue before sliding it inside to dance with hers.

She put one hand around his neck, the other on his chest, tested the springiness of the few hairs that had escaped the confinement of his shirt. Then, giving in to her long-standing impulse to tangle her fingers in the unruly mat, she tugged at the button.

It popped off.

She jerked away, looking at him in horror.

"It's okay," he assured her. "The laundry can sew it back on."

She bent over, searching for the small white object. It must have bounced on the hardwood floor. It could be anywhere! She'd have to spend forever looking for it. What lousy timing!

His hands on her shoulders tugged her back until she was facing him again. "What are you doing?"

"Looking for your button."

"It's all right," he reassured her. "They're generic. The laundry has plenty. Forget it."

"Oh. Okay." But the mood had been interrupted. What should she do now? She really wanted to pick up where they'd left off but wasn't sure how to go about suggesting it.

His eyes lowered, focusing on her mouth. Apparently he wanted the same thing, and he had no problem deciding how to proceed. With a groan, he pulled her close.

"Emily," he whispered, his lips moving, speaking the words against hers, "do you have any idea what you're doing to me?"

"Making you feel incredibly wonderful, I hope," she whispered back. "That's what you're doing to me."

He moved a hand between them, tentatively circling her breast with one finger, brushing the turgid nipple gently, as if accidentally, giving her every chance to protest. For an answer, she slid her fingers through his chest hairs now exposed by the missing button, felt the rapid pounding of his heart, massaged the hard muscles she found there.

"Oh, Emily," he moaned, and pulled a few inches away. He looked deeply into her eyes, searching her face. In the gathering darkness his own gaze glowed like green fire.

He stood and, in a swift gesture, lifted her in his arms. She gasped in surprise, then nestled against him. It seemed appropriate; he'd been supporting her all evening.

In a few strides they were in the bedroom. Briefly she wished she'd made the bed that morning, but as he laid her down and bent over to kiss her, that concern lost any priority.

He dropped onto the bed beside her—and started a tidal wave. His hands gripped her arms, and she laughed.

"Relax," she said. "You'll get used to it. Just try to avoid sudden moves."

"I can do that. We'll take every movement very slowly," he whispered, his voice husky with promise as he pulled her on top of him, his lips finding hers again.

His mouth was soft and warm against hers, his body solid and hard beneath her. The motion of the water raised and lowered them, as though they were already making love, and she surrendered herself to the exquisite sensations.

She was wrinkling his shirt, his pants, probably beyond repair, but he didn't seem to mind. In fact, he was pretty busy rumpling her clothing, pushing her T-shirt up, caressing her skin, sending the blood boiling through her veins.

He rolled them over so they were side by side, and created another tidal wave.

"Will I ever get used to this?" he groaned, trying to steady himself on his elbows and making matters worse.

"You'll love it when you get into the rhythm," she promised.

"I'm counting on it." Balancing precariously, he pushed her shirt up, exposing her breasts, and lowered his head.

And the doorbell rang.

"Ignore it," he begged, touching her nipple with his tongue, sending bolts of lightning through her entire body.

She hesitated, wanting desperately to plunge back into the most incredible passion she'd ever experienced, to make love with him.

But...

"I can't. It might be important," she moaned, though she made no move to free herself from his tantalizing mouth.

"More important than this?" He trailed kisses down the side of her breast, over to the other one, ending with its nipple.

She groaned as her body seemed to take on a life of its own. Could anything be more important than what they were doing?

The damn doorbell shrieked again.

He muttered a curse and lifted his head. "I should have disconnected that thing when I took the phone off the hook."

"What?" She sat bolt upright, pulling away from him. "You took my phone off the hook?"

He lay on his stomach, blinking dazedly, uncomprehendingly.

She rolled off the bed and began straightening her clothes with angry jerks. "You did it when you reached around me for something on the end table. Of course."

"Emily..." He floundered on the water bed, trying to get up, fighting the rolling motion instead of moving with it. "Emily, somebody always interrupts us. We can't do anything without somebody calling or coming by. Don't you think this is one time you can be without your never-ending supply of friends?" His words sent fragments of ice through her veins, replacing the fire he'd so recently created.

"That's not your decision to make. You had no right to take my phone off the hook and try to separate me from my friends."

He flopped out of the bed and stood facing her. "It's obvious no one could ever do that. Your friends are all you need, and apparently I'm not even on the list."

The doorbell rang twice in quick succession followed by a pounding.

Emily straightened her shoulders and thrust out her chin. "You could be on the list. You just can't be the only one. Don't ask me to choose between you and my friends. I do need them, all of them, anytime."

"I see," he said curtly.

"No, you don't." She turned her back on him and went to answer the door.

As soon as she saw who stood on the porch, her heart sank and she almost wished she'd listened to Carson. Susie could talk nonstop for hours without ever saying anything of importance.

"I had to come over. The operator said your phone was off the hook. You won't believe what's happened."

Emoting dramatically, Susie followed Emily back into the room, but Emily didn't hear her words. *I see,* Carson had said, but he didn't. He'd never experienced the pain of losing everybody you loved at once, of being all alone. She needed people who cared about her. She needed every friend she had and then some. If Carson couldn't handle that, and he obviously couldn't, she had no room in her life for him.

"Am I interrupting something?" Susie asked when he came into the room, then immediately continued her story without waiting for an answer.

Carson crossed the room, retrieved his shoes and socks and came up beside her. He looked at her for an eternal moment, then at Susie, and walked out.

She had to consciously order her feet to remain in place, not to follow him. Pain and loneliness surged inside her as the door closed behind him. But it didn't matter, she assured herself. She still had her friends, lots of friends. This aching alone feeling was only temporary. It would go away as soon as she connected with Sam and Celia and Paula and Nora and Julia....

Chapter Ten

Emily slid into the miniature race car and prepared to take her turn to see if she could beat Sam's best time. Of the six of them who'd come to the Malibu Grand Prix racetrack this evening, Sam was ahead so far—naturally, since he drove in real races. But Emily had been known to beat his time in the miniatures, making up in daring what she lacked in skill.

But tonight she found her mind wandering, and she spun out on the second curve. Damn! It was Carson's fault. He'd been haunting her all week, no matter how much fun she was having.

She pulled up to the finish line and climbed out, unbuckling her helmet.

Sam rushed up. "Hey! You've got two more laps."

"You take them. I'm just not in the mood."

Sam signaled for Pat to come up and take the extra tickets. Draping an arm around Emily's shoulders, he led her over to one side of the stands. "What's the matter, kiddo? You've been acting strange all week."

"Nothing." Even as she said the word, she marveled that she would lie to Sam. They'd never had any secrets. But somehow this just wasn't something she could share with him ... or anyone else for that matter. Not even if she completely understood what was happening to her. And she didn't.

Everywhere she went, she took thoughts of Carson with her—the mischievous look in his eyes when they'd had their mud fight, the sensual way he'd lowered his lips to hers, the way his hands had felt on her body, the way his body had felt beneath her fingers ... everything about him. No matter how many friends she surrounded herself with, she sensed a gap, an empty hole just Carson's size.

The whole thing made no sense whatsoever.

"Something," Sam said, denying her assertion that nothing was wrong. "I know you too well. Something's definitely wrong. And when you're ready to talk about it, you know I'm here."

He pulled her close for a brotherly hug ... but the embrace didn't bring the comfort it always had before. The arms were the wrong arms. They didn't belong to Carson.

Saturday morning dawned bright, sunny and crystalline clear. Not a cloud in sight. Hell, no. They were all hanging directly over Carson's head, raining down on him.

He leaned against his front balcony door, sipping his coffee, peering out, wishing for a storm. In a raging downpour, maybe he could sit outside and have his coffee. But this weather was like an irritating Pollyanna—laughing and dancing when there was nothing to laugh or dance about.

He tensed as the door slammed downstairs and realized that was what he'd been waiting for. As soon as Emily left, he could go out on his balcony and indulge his weekend routine. He just didn't want to see her—more unwelcome sunshine.

Since their disastrous evening, she'd resumed her normal activities with what seemed to him like a determined frenzy—determined to prove to him and maybe to herself that she didn't need a one-on-one relationship. Well, he believed her. She could stop anytime.

On the other hand, at least when she was gone with her friends all the time he didn't have to think about her being directly beneath him, didn't have to fight off a desire to go down and grab her and carry her off to a desert island.

Except for those times when he woke in the middle of the night and knew she must surely be home and he couldn't go back to sleep until nearly dawn. Somehow, with her spontaneous, adventurous approach to life, her big heart that took in everybody she met, and her happy smile, she'd gotten under his skin—way under. Down to his toes, his fingertips—his heart.

In spite of his efforts to resist, she'd brought fun back into his life, reminded him of forgotten pleasures like the feel of mud between his fingers and the wonder of watching a maple seed swirl through the air or a lightning bug blink.

But it would never work. While he had no doubt she cared for him, too, he knew that she cared for everybody...equally. And he didn't want her to love him the same way she loved Sam and Celia and Jeremy and half the world. He wanted her to love him the way a woman loves the only man in her life.

The way he loved her. Much as he hated to admit it, he did love her, and getting her out of his system was going to be tough.

Now he stood inside his house, waiting for the sound of her turquoise turtle to signal her departure. When it didn't come, he stepped out onto the balcony. She stood beside the car, arms folded under her breasts, looking down with a forlorn expression.

Without thinking, he moved to the rail and peered down at her. "What's the matter?"

She jumped, looked up at him, and for a brief instant a bright smile spread over her face, landing smack in the middle of his heart. Then immediately her scowl returned. "Flat tire. I've been putting air in it every morning, but now it's so flat I can't drive it to the service station."

She looked desolate, helpless. Of course she was helpless, he reminded himself. Without her flock of friends, she was lost. And with a flat tire, she couldn't get to them.

Which meant they'd have to come to her and disrupt his day. That was, he assured himself, the only reason he offered to change the damn tire.

"Oh, no," she protested. "You can't do that."

"Of course I can." He had to resist a sudden impulse to swing over the balcony and drop to the ground the way he'd seen it done in the movies and had always wanted to try. She did that to him, made him want to attempt crazy things, things he wouldn't ordinarily even think about doing.

Instead he turned away and strode back into the house, ignoring her further protestations. He marched down the stairs and out to her.

She didn't look very happy to see him, and he felt even more dejected at her lack of enthusiasm. Not only had he failed to achieve a special place in her life, but apparently he didn't even rank up there with her fifty closest friends.

"Okay," he said, brushing his hands together briskly, "where's your jack? Do you own a jack?"

"There's no point in—"

"Never mind. I'll get mine out of the garage." No point? There was a damn big point to getting her tire fixed and getting her out of there. For one thing, if he had to stand beside her for one more minute, he'd pull her into his arms and tell her everything was going to be all right. Hell, he'd probably give her the keys to his own car if he thought it would bring the smile back to her face.

Crazy.

"No..." She restrained him with a slim hand on his bare arm as he started in the direction of the garage.

A bolt of lightning shot through him at her touch, bringing desire, warmth.... It felt too good. He jerked his arm back, then regretted his action when her golden eyes darkened with hurt.

Damn! What did she expect, anyway? How much did she think he could take?

She smiled a tiny half smile and shrugged. "I have a jack. I just don't have a spare tire. Well, I *do* have a spare tire. It's the one on the car that's flat. The tire that's in my trunk now was the flat one I replaced with the spare. I never got around to getting it fixed."

"So you've been driving all week with no spare, getting this tire aired up rather than having it repaired." He threw his arms into the air. "Do you know how ridiculous that is?"

The hurt look changed to anger, and he preferred that. "I've been busy! I haven't had time."

"Right. Busy charging around like a maniac, trying to see how many people you can wedge into one week."

She glared at him and whirled away, heading for the house.

Instantly he wished he could take back his angry words. "I'm sorry," he called after her. "Look, I'll take you wherever you need to go."

She hesitated, one foot on the step and the other on the sidewalk. "That's okay," she said, her back to him, her voice pitched a shade higher than normal. "I'll, uh, just go call somebody."

"Calling one of your friends to drive all the way over here and pick you up would be ridiculous when I'm here already." He found himself resenting the fact that she'd refuse his help then ask someone else. "I don't mind taking you wherever you want to go. I have the whole morning free."

"Oh, well, my plans weren't very important. I could just cancel them." She still had her back toward him, and her voice had a desperate quality. Something was wrong. This wasn't like Emily. She was hiding something, though he couldn't imagine what.

He moved up slowly behind her, so close her scent of wildflowers reached up to him and he felt warmth emanating from her skin as though she'd stored the sun's rays in her tan. "There's no need for that. I insist on taking you," he said. "Where do we need to go? What are your plans, Emily?"

She leapt the rest of the way onto the porch, turning slowly to face him, legs wide apart, hands on her hips and chin thrust forward. "Roller skating," she said. Defiantly, he thought. "I'm going roller skating with some friends."

"Okay," he said, puzzled that she seemed so defensive about the activity. It sounded like fun. He'd enjoyed roller skating when Celia used to take him years ago.

To his surprise, he found himself wanting Emily to invite him to come along, to include him in her group, in her fun. "I'll go upstairs and get my keys, then take you wherever you need to go," he said briskly, banishing his erratic thoughts.

She grimaced, her defiance fading. "I don't think that's such a good idea."

"Why?"

Since they'd been standing outside for a good fifteen minutes, it didn't surprise Carson when her phone began to ring. It was overdue.

"I gotta answer that. 'Bye."

Emily dashed inside and snatched up the phone, thankful for the excuse to get away from Carson's questions.

"Emily, I think I'm going to have to cancel our plans." Celia's voice was so weak Emily barely recognized it.

Emily's immediate response was relief that she wouldn't have to take Celia along to do something the older woman probably shouldn't be doing or to deal with Carson's anger should he find out. "No problem. I've got a flat tire, anyway. Is everything okay?"

"Everything's fine. I just don't feel quite up to par this morning."

"You're sick? What's the matter?"

"Nothing, really. I have a slight headache, but mostly I'm just exhausted. I didn't sleep very well last night."

Emily frowned. "As soon as I can get something done about this tire, I'll be over to check on you."

"That's not neces—"

Emily heard a clattering noise, as if the phone had been dropped, then silence.

"Celia? Are you there? Celia?" They'd been disconnected, that's all, she told herself, but a disconnect sound didn't clatter. A cold wind wrapped around her, piercing to her heart as she recalled the night her parents and grandparents had been late coming home. Her baby-sitter had been unconcerned, had assured her they'd probably stopped for a drink or, at the worst, had car trouble. But that hadn't been the worst. What if something had happened to Celia? Carson had warned her. If Celia was ill... or worse... she'd never forgive herself.

She hung up the phone, then picked it up and dialed Celia's number, praying Celia would answer and they could complain about the unreliable telephone service.

But all she got was a busy signal.

Heart pounding erratically, she dashed outside to where Carson waited, standing stiffly erect, tossing and catching his car keys.

"Something's happened to Celia," she gasped, trying to keep the panic at bay. "We've got to get over there."

He caught the keys, clenching them in his fist. His eyes flared wide in the panic she was fighting. "What do you mean, something's happened? What?"

Emily shook her head. "I don't know. She said she didn't feel well, then we got cut off or she dropped the phone or something, but she wouldn't answer me. I called back and got a busy signal. Let's go!" How could he just stand there?

"First we call the retirement village to go check on her," he said, brushing past her and heading upstairs, taking the steps two at a time.

Emily went back inside and tried again to call Celia, with the same results.

She ran back out in time to see Carson striding off the porch. Determined not to be left behind, she ran after him, across the yard and down the driveway to the garage. Without waiting for an invitation, she climbed into the passenger side of his car.

He looked at her, and she lifted her chin, preparing to defend her right to go along. But instead of protesting, he took her hand. "It's probably nothing," he assured her. "Just bad phone service. Even if something did happen, she'll get immediate care. That's one of the benefits of her being there." But in spite of his sensible words, she noted even in the gloom of the garage that his eyes were dark with fear.

She squeezed his hand. "I know. Just a glitch in the telephone service." *Like my family just stopped for a drink.* The thought rose unbidden to torment her.

"The telephone company is notorious for that sort of thing." His gaze, his hand, his presence—all held her firmly. "This isn't like the time you lost your family," he said, as if reading her mind. She sensed he was reassuring himself as much as her.

He started the car and backed out of the garage.

"The door," she reminded him when they were halfway down the drive.

He hit the remote control to lower the door.

Meticulous Carson Thayer had almost driven off and left his garage door open. That small act of neglect told her he was as worried as she.

She took his arm and held it tightly. At first she thought he might jerk it away from her as he'd done earlier, but instead he clasped one hand over hers.

It was enough. She knew he was accepting what little comfort she could give, and his acceptance was comforting to her. Still, her heart pounded in fear and her stomach clenched painfully.

"What happened when your family died?" he asked, careering around a corner. Equally as telling as forgetting the garage door was the fact that he was breaking every speed limit and even ran a stop sign on his way to his grandmother.

"They went to a dinner party, leaving me with a sitter," she answered, amazed at how vivid and painful the memory suddenly was. Until a few minutes ago she'd thought it was too far in the past to keep hurting. "I got mad because they were going without me. I almost refused to kiss them goodbye, but at the last minute I ran after them just before they went out the door. Mama held me extra tight that night. I've always wondered if somehow she knew." She paused and bit her lip. "That's all. They never came home. A drunk driver ran a red light and smashed into their car."

"And left you alone."

She nodded, even though she knew he was watching the road and not her.

"That's not going to happen today." She wasn't sure if he was talking to her or to himself. "After all," he said, a tight, artificial smile stretching his mouth, "a drunk driver couldn't possibly get into Grandmother's house. She has far too much furniture in there."

Emily produced a laugh for his benefit, but it was as artificial as his smile.

Carson's finger tapped the steering wheel as he waited impatiently at a traffic signal.

"You really care about my grandmother, don't you?" he asked.

"Of course I do. She's my friend, and that means a lot to me."

The light changed to green, and he pulled away, passing a slower car.

"I've come to realize that, Emily, but people aren't interchangeable, you know."

The first part of his statement sent a beam of light through the darkness of her worry. He understood about her friends. But the second part brought a frown to her face. "What are you talking about? Whoever said they were?"

"Your family died and left you all alone. So now you fill your life with a crowd of friends so you'll never have to be alone again."

She considered his assessment. "Is that so awful?" she asked.

"No, not at all. Except you need to think about it. If anything should happen to Celia—and one day it will—do you think it will hurt any less because you have other friends? People you care about aren't like tires—if one goes flat, you put on another. The loss of each one is going to hurt, no matter how many remain."

The air around Emily blurred and shimmered, and she felt weak with fear—fear for Celia, fear of the pain of loss, and fear for Carson. He was right, of course. Much as she valued her widespread family, it was no guarantee against pain. If anything happened to Celia—but she wouldn't think about that. She hung on to Carson's arm. "Nothing's going to happen to Celia—not for a long time," she said for his benefit as well as her own.

Carson swung into the retirement village and pulled up in front of Celia's unit, braking sharply, parking illegally. With one motion he switched off the engine and yanked the keys from the ignition, then paused and turned to her. His eyes were filled with so many contradictory emotions—fear and trust, strength and need, despair and hope—that Emily was sure she'd never again think of him as "scrunched up inside."

"I'm glad you're with me," he said softly.

Before she could respond, he was out of the car and halfway up the walk. She hurried to catch up with him, but he paused at the door, waiting for her before he rang the bell.

A nurse in a white uniform answered his ring. Emily's heart lurched into her throat and she felt Carson's hand close around hers.

"I'm looking for Celia Thayer," he said, his voice strong, betraying none of the inner turmoil she knew he was feeling.

"Is that you, Carson?" The nurse stepped back as Celia's voice came from inside the unit.

"Grandmother!" Carson pushed in with Emily close behind.

Celia, clad in a white robe, struggled to a sitting position on the sofa where she'd been lying. "And Emily. How nice to see you."

"Grandmother, are you all right?" Carson looked from Celia to the nurse.

"She's fine," the woman replied, and Emily felt a large weight lift from her shoulders. "She just needs some rest."

"Of course I'm all right," Celia said, her tired voice firm. "Why wouldn't I be?"

Carson strode across the room to sit beside her. "What happened? You were talking to Emily, and the line went dead."

"Oh, that." She waved a wrinkled hand toward an end table where a portable phone lay, its plastic casing split open. "The blasted thing slipped right out of my fingers, fell on the floor and came apart."

"I tried to call you back and got a busy signal," Emily said, sinking into a chair, her legs rubbery with relief. However, that relief mingled with a trace of embarrassment that she'd gotten so upset—and gotten Carson so upset—over nothing.

"It took me a while to figure out that I had to disconnect the entire portable phone setup before my other phones would work," Celia explained.

"Mrs. Thayer," the nurse interrupted, "you get some rest, and I'll check on you this afternoon."

"I don't need to be checked on."

"Nevertheless, I'll be back." The woman left with a smile, closing the door behind her.

Celia sighed. "Carson, dear, I wish you hadn't called the management. They came charging in here like I'd had a heart attack."

"Good. That's what they're supposed to do. For all we knew, you could have had a heart attack. We were worried about you."

"I'm sorry." She looked at Emily and lifted a hand to her mouth. "Oh, Emily, you missed your roller skating."

"That's okay. I'm just glad you're all right."

"A good night's sleep and I'll be better than new. Perhaps we could reschedule our skating for next week since you missed it, too."

Emily cringed as Carson shot up off the sofa.

"You were taking my grandmother roller skating?" he exclaimed.

"You leave Emily alone. I asked to go along with her," Celia corrected. "I'm an excellent skater. In case you've forgotten, I taught you."

Carson glowered at Emily, then looked back to Celia. "That was more than a few years ago, Grandmother. You're a little older now."

Celia folded her arms, her pale eyes flashing. "Sweetheart, I'm really getting tired of your constantly reminding me how old I am. I don't feel like an old woman, and I intend to have fun and enjoy whatever years I have left, whether that's two or twenty. Emily's reminded me of the joy of living. You might take a few lessons and stop acting like an old man. Don't let the best thing that's ever happened to you get away." She narrowed her eyes at her grandson, then turned to Emily. "Forgive me, my dear—" She didn't look at all apologetic. "I'm afraid I—what's the term?—*set you up* with my grandson. He needs someone like you, and I knew you wouldn't be able to resist the challenge when I told you he was beyond help."

"G-Grandmother!" Carson sputtered.

Emily's jaw dropped. "Celia!" she protested. "You *wanted* me to... to..." *Tear up his newspaper? Break his window?* Come to need him, to care for him when the whole situation was ridiculously impossible?

Celia smoothed the sofa cushion beside her. "And you need him," she continued unconcernedly. "A stabilizing factor in your fun-filled if slightly erratic life. Someone to love body and soul instead of trying to surround yourself with a thousand friends who, wonderful as they are, can never quite touch that special place in your heart."

Emily could only stare in stunned silence at the woman who, after delivering such outrageous pronouncements, was calmly leaning back on her sofa, looking pleased with herself. She couldn't even blame Celia's age, accuse her of senility. Her words hit home. She was right.

Emily did need Carson. He did, indeed, fill that empty space she'd never completely been able to fill no matter how many friends she had. All week she'd been with her friends, and all week she'd felt alone.

She noticed Carson wasn't saying anything, either. Apparently he was as shocked as she.

After an eternity, Carson cleared his throat. "Excuse us, Grandmother," he said. "We'll leave you alone while you rest." He rose, extending a hand to Emily. She stood, too, and, with a hand at the small of her back, Carson pushed her out the door. Closing it behind them, he grabbed her arm to stop her, yanking her around to face him.

"Roller skating?" he demanded, totally and, she suspected, deliberately ignoring Celia's revelation. "You're both nuts!"

She looked at the sidewalk, then back to him defiantly. "She asked to go with me. I didn't know how to say no. I couldn't tell her she was too old."

"You certainly could have. She *is* too old. You can wish it away all you want, but the reality is, Grandmother's eighty-four years old. Her reaction time is slower than yours, her bones are brittle. She could end up with a broken hip and never walk again." His anger blazed so hot she could almost feel the heat searing her heart.

"If I couldn't talk her out of it, I'd planned to stick right beside her and be sure she didn't fall," Emily defended, yanking her arm from his grasp.

He sighed, stepped away from her and jammed his hands onto his hips. "What if you both fell? You never think about the consequences, do you?"

"I don't spend so much time worrying about what might happen that I never do anything, if that's what you mean."

He looked at her strangely. "Oh, you do things, all right. You surround yourself with as many people as possible. Why? I know. So you'll never have to be alone. But why so many? So you don't run the risk of getting too close to any one of us? So everybody stays just a friend? So you always have a backup ready if you lose somebody? I told you, that doesn't work with people you care about."

She shook her head, dismayed by the brutal turn their discussion had taken after they'd been so close on the trip over. "My friends are an important part of my life."

"I know. Boy, do I know. Come on." He opened the passenger door of his car and waved her in. "I can drop you at the roller rink so you can meet your friends, or take you home so you can call them. Whatever you want. I love you, but I can't compete with all your friends." He turned away and walked to the other side of the car.

She stood staring after him, stunned. *I love you?* It was the worst profession of love she'd ever heard. He'd offered it with one hand and snatched it away with the other.

She'd felt so close to him as they'd shared their concern about Celia and rushed to her aid even if it had been a false alarm. Now he'd taken all that away at the same time he'd tossed out his declaration of love. With only a small ripple of surprise, she admitted to herself that his words had found an echo in her. She loved him, and she wasn't about to let him get away so easily. She slid into the car beside him.

"Can we go somewhere and talk?" she asked.

"Anywhere you want. What'll it be? The roller rink? Sam's house?"

"Somewhere alone." He wasn't going to make this easy.

He raised one eyebrow. "Alone? Just you and me? No friends? No telephone? Are you sure you can handle that?"

"You don't need to be sarcastic."

"All right," he capitulated. "Let's grab something to eat and go to the park."

He started the car and pulled away from the curb, then stopped so abruptly she lurched forward, her seat belt restraining her. As he looked at her, she thought she saw a softening on his face and in his eyes ... but not in his voice. "No pizza," he snapped, then turned his attention again to driving.

"Did I mention pizza?" Though, as her favorite comfort food, that was what she'd immediately thought of when he'd mentioned eating. Maybe she could talk him into tacos with extra hot sauce.

Half an hour later they arrived at the park near Celia's old home, the park where she'd blown dandelion seeds in his hair and he'd kissed her for the first time. The afternoon was perfect, warm and bright with a gentle breeze slowly moving tufts of clouds across the blue sky. A few kids were batting around a baseball at the far end, but the rest of the park belonged to them.

Together they walked over to the swings and sat down next to each other. Emily unwrapped her sandwich. Corned beef with mustard. He hadn't gone for the tacos.

She took a bite. Not too bad.

She kicked off her shoes and pushed on the well-packed earth, rocking the swing back and forth, then looked over at Carson. He was concentrating on his sandwich, sitting perfectly still. His navy shorts and white knit shirt were immaculate, but he himself appeared a little wrinkled.

Then, as if he could feel her gaze on him, he looked up, and there it was in his eyes, as clear as the day around them. He did love her. But he was holding it back, keeping his emotions in control.

"Carson," she said, feeling uncomfortable as always at his reserve. "I'm really sorry about the roller skating. You know I'd never do anything to hurt Celia." She took a sip of her drink, stirred the ice with her straw. "She assured me she was an excellent skater. She once skated as part of her dance routine. Okay, so that was a few years ago. She wanted to go so badly, I didn't have the heart to tell her she couldn't enjoy herself. Somehow I'd have figured out a way to keep her from falling. You know I would have."

"Yes," he admitted. "Somehow I have every confidence you'll do whatever you set out to do." He cleared his throat, studied his sandwich so intently she found herself looking at it for signs that the corned beef was about to speak or tap dance. "I guess I can understand her point," he finally continued, "about wanting to have fun as long as she can. So maybe you could steer her into exciting but less physical activities."

Her feet froze in midpush, and she almost tumbled forward. She stared at him in amazement for a minute, replaying his words in her mind to make sure she'd heard them right. He was accepting the relationship between Celia and her, the fact that Celia would likely be indulging in some activities not offered at the retirement village. "Well, uh, yeah, I guess so. Sure." She hesitated, then decided to push it to the limit. "You might want to join us sometime. Since you see your grandmother's point."

He studied her the way he'd studied his sandwich a minute before. "I might."

Well. Would wonders never cease? Maybe they could take up skydiving together—she'd always wanted to try that—and Celia could learn to fly the plane. With his meticulous bent, he'd be great at folding the parachutes.

She took another bite of her sandwich. It was tasting better all the time. A butterfly lit on the back of her hand, fanned its yellow wings a couple of times as if in greeting, then flitted away, playing on the warm breezes. She watched its progress with fascination, feeling a camaraderie.

"Carson, about my friends..." she began, deciding to jump in headfirst.

He stiffened. "What about them?"

"Well, they're really important to me."

"I know that." His tone grated and his gaze became wary.

"I've never liked being alone, but lately, I've felt alone even when I was with someone." She swallowed hard and forced herself to continue, to leave herself wide open and vulnerable. "It's like Celia said. You fill the empty spot in a way nobody else does. I love you different from how I love my friends. All week I've needed to be with *you*, not anybody else. Nobody else would do, and goodness knows I tried!"

He grabbed the cable of her swing, stopping her motion. "You think there's any chance that sort of thing might happen again?"

She searched the depths of his leaf green eyes. Finding what she sought, she smiled. "Maybe."

"I'm willing to concede that friends are necessary. But I don't want to have to share you all the time with everybody in the city."

She considered that for a moment, then nodded. "Okay. Maybe sometimes we could take the phone off the hook," she teased. "Or let the answering machine pick up."

"And disconnect the doorbell, at least while we're making love." His eyes sparkled and his lips tilted upward.

"Only if we get one of those signs for the front door that says 'Back At' a certain time."

He scowled.

"I'm kidding," she said. He still had a few things to learn but, after all, she was a teacher.

He reached over and took her hand, his thumb massaging her knuckles as he studied it intently before looking at her again. "I have to admit, you've brought fun back into my life, taught me to look at the world with the wonder of a child. There's so much out there I want to do, and I want to share it all with you. But I don't want to be your generic friend. I don't want to be interchangeable with dozens of other people. I want you to know that you belong to me and me to you always, even when we're not together physically. I love you. I want a specific place in your family of friends. I want to be a husband to you and a father to your children."

The late afternoon sun must have left the sky; she could feel it exploding inside her, filling her with sunshine. But—

"I want to adopt all the unwanted children in the world," she explained, dreading his reaction but knowing it had to be said. To her surprise, he didn't pull back into his shell. His only visible reaction was a grimace. Not so bad.

"I understand you *want* to," he said patiently, "but you can't. Will you settle for two or three and a couple of our own?"

"How about three or four?"

"If we bought Grandmother's old house, I suppose we'd have room."

Tears sprang to her eyes. "Celia's old house? We can live where your family's lived for generations. Our kids can raise their kids there. A real ancestral home!" She flung her arms around him, smashing her sandwich against his back. "Oh, dear." She withdrew, clutching the mashed mess of bread, meat and mustard.

"It's okay," he assured her. "I've just got to quit wearing white."

He pulled her swing closer to his, leaned over and kissed her, slowly, tantalizingly. She returned the kiss, boldly, crazily, tossing her sandwich aside this time before she wrapped both arms around him. As he deepened the kiss, she fervently wished them at home with the phone off the hook and the doorbell disconnected.

She felt like a maple seed whirling and spinning ecstatically—except she knew she'd never touch the ground again.

*   *   *   *   *

COMING NEXT MONTH

#1102 ALWAYS DADDY—Karen Rose Smith
Bundles of Joy—Make Believe Marriage
Jonathan Wescott thought money could buy anything. But lovely
Alicia Fallon, the adoptive mother of his newfound baby daughter,
couldn't be bought. And before he knew it, he was longing for the
right to love not only his little girl, but also her mother!

#1103 COLTRAIN'S PROPOSAL—Diana Palmer
Make Believe Marriage
Coltrain had made some mistakes in life, but loving Louise Blakely
wasn't one of them. So when Louise prepared to leave town, cajoling
her into a fake engagement to help his image *seemed* like a good idea.
But now Coltrain had to convince her that it wasn't his image he cared
for, but Louise herself!

#1104 GREEN CARD WIFE—Anne Peters
Make Believe Marriage—First Comes Marriage
Silka Katarina Olsen gladly agreed to a platonic marriage with
Ted Carstairs—it would allow her to work in the States and gain her
citizenship. But soon Silka found herself with unfamiliar feelings
for Ted that made their convenient arrangement very complicated!

#1105 ALMOST A HUSBAND—Carol Grace
Make Believe Marriage
Carrie Stephens was tired of big-city life with its big problems.
She wanted to escape it, and a hopeless passion for her partner,
Matt Graham. But when Matt posed as her fiancé for her new job,
Carrie doubted if distance would ever make her truly forget how
she loved him....

#1106 DREAM BRIDE—Terri Lindsey
Make Believe Marriage
Gloria Hamilton would only marry a man who cared for *her,* not just
her sophisticated ways. So when Luke Cahill trumpeted about his
qualifications for the perfect bride, Gloria decided to give Luke some
lessons of her own...in love!

#1107 THE GROOM MAKER—Lisa Kaye Laurel
Make Believe Marriage
Rae Browning had lots of dates—they just ended up marrying
someone else! So when sworn bachelor Trent Colton bet that she
couldn't turn him into a groom, Rae knew she had a sure deal. The
problem was, the only person she wanted Trent to marry was herself!

SOMETIMES BIG SURPRISES
COME IN SMALL PACKAGES!

BABY TALK
Julianna Morris

Cassie Cavannaugh wanted a baby, without the complications of an affair. But somehow she couldn't forget sexy Jake O'Connor, or the idea that he could father her child. Jake was handsome, headstrong, unpredictable...and nothing but trouble. But every time she got close to Jake, playing it smart seemed a losing battle....

Coming in August 1995 from

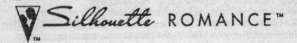

BOJ3

HE'S MORE THAN A MAN, HE'S ONE OF OUR

ALWAYS DADDY
Karen Rose Smith

Alicia Fallon's daughter was the most important part of her life. So when charming Jonathan Wescott appeared to claim his child, Alicia was ready for a fight. But was there no defense against her own hidden passion for this wealthy rogue?

Look for *Always Daddy* by Karen Rose Smith, available in September from Silhouette Romance.

Fall in love with our Fabulous Fathers!

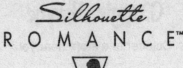

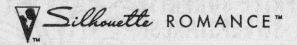

Silhouette ROMANCE™

Silhouette Romance is proud to present a new series by
Anne Peters

first Comes Marriage

GREEN CARD WIFE
Anne Peters

Sika Olsen knew her marriage to Ted Carstairs was in name only.
She would get a green card, Ted would get a substantial fee and
both of them would be happy. Until Silka found herself wishing their
arrangement could be more than just a "paper" marriage.

First Comes Marriage...will love follow?
Starting in September 1995.

FCM-1

PRIZE SURPRISE SWEEPSTAKES!

This month's prize:

BEAUTIFUL WEDGWOOD CHINA!

This month, as a special surprise, we're giving away a bone china dinner service for eight by Wedgwood**, one of England's most prestigious manufacturers!

Think how beautiful your table will look, set with lovely Wedgwood china in the casual Countryware pattern! Each five-piece place setting includes dinner plate, salad plate, soup bowl and cup and saucer.

The facing page contains two Entry Coupons (as does every book you received this shipment). Complete and return *all* the entry coupons; **the more times you enter, the better your chances of winning!**

Then keep your fingers crossed, because you'll find out by September 15, 1995 if you're the winner!

Remember: The more times you enter, the better your chances of winning!*

PRIZE SURPRISE
SWEEPSTAKES

OFFICIAL ENTRY COUPON

This entry must be received by: AUGUST 30, 1995
This month's winner will be notified by: SEPTEMBER 15, 1995

YES, I want to win the Wedgwood china service for eight! Please enter me in the drawing and let me know if I've won!

Name_____

Address _____ Apt. _____

City   State/Prov.   Zip/Postal Code

Account #_____

Return entry with invoice in reply envelope.

© 1995 HARLEQUIN ENTERPRISES LTD.   CWW KAL

PRIZE SURPRISE
SWEEPSTAKES

OFFICIAL ENTRY COUPON

This entry must be received by: AUGUST 30, 1995
This month's winner will be notified by: SEPTEMBER 15, 1995

YES, I want to win the Wedgwood china service for eight! Please enter me in the drawing and let me know if I've won!

Name_____

Address _____ Apt. _____

City   State/Prov.   Zip/Postal Code

Account #_____

Return entry with invoice in reply envelope.

© 1995 HARLEQUIN ENTERPRISES LTD.   CWW KAL

OFFICIAL RULES

PRIZE SURPRISE SWEEPSTAKES 3448

NO PURCHASE OR OBLIGATION NECESSARY

Three Harlequin Reader Service 1995 shipments will contain respectively, coupons for entry into three different prize drawings, one for a Panasonic 31" wide-screen TV, another for a 5-piece Wedgwood china service for eight and the third for a Sharp ViewCam camcorder. To enter any drawing using an Entry Coupon, simply complete and mail according to directions.

There is no obligation to continue using the Reader Service to enter and be eligible for any prize drawing. You may also enter any drawing by hand printing the words "Prize Surprise," your name and address on a 3"x5" card and the name of the prize you wish that entry to be considered for (i.e., Panasonic wide-screen TV, Wedgwood china or Sharp ViewCam). Send your 3"x5" entries via first-class mail (limit: one per envelope) to: Prize Surprise Sweepstakes 3448, c/o the prize you wish that entry to be considered for, P.O. Box 1315, Buffalo, NY 14269-1315, USA or P.O. Box 610, Fort Erie, Ontario L2A 5X3, Canada.

To be eligible for the Panasonic wide-screen TV, entries must be received by 6/30/95; for the Wedgwood china, 8/30/95; and for the Sharp ViewCam, 10/30/95.

Winners will be determined in random drawings conducted under the supervision of D.L. Blair, Inc., an independent judging organization whose decisions are final, from among all eligible entries received for that drawing. Approximate prize values are as follows: Panasonic wide-screen TV ($1,800); Wedgwood china ($840) and Sharp ViewCam ($2,000). Sweepstakes open to residents of the U.S. (except Puerto Rico) and Canada, 18 years of age or older. Employees and immediate family members of Harlequin Enterprises, Ltd., D.L. Blair, Inc., their affiliates, subsidiaries and all other agencies, entities and persons connected with the use, marketing or conduct of this sweepstakes are not eligible. Odds of winning a prize are dependent upon the number of eligible entries received for that drawing. Prize drawing and winner notification for each drawing will occur no later than 15 days after deadline for entry eligibility for that drawing. Limit: one prize to an individual, family or organization. All applicable laws and regulations apply. Sweepstakes offer void wherever prohibited by law. Any litigation within the province of Quebec respecting the conduct and awarding of the prizes in this sweepstakes must be submitted to the Regies des loteries et Courses du Quebec. In order to win a prize, residents of Canada will be required to correctly answer a time-limited arithmetical skill-testing question. Value of prizes are in U.S. currency.

Winners will be obligated to sign and return an Affidavit of Eligibility within 30 days of notification. In the event of noncompliance within this time period, prize may not be awarded. If any prize or prize notification is returned as undeliverable, that prize will not be awarded. By acceptance of a prize, winner consents to use of his/her name, photograph or other likeness for purposes of advertising, trade and promotion on behalf of Harlequin Enterprises, Ltd., without further compensation, unless prohibited by law.

For the names of prizewinners (available after 12/31/95), send a self-addressed, stamped envelope to: Prize Surprise Sweepstakes 3448 Winners, P.O. Box 4200, Blair, NE 68009.

RPZ KAL